# THE FLOOD

# THE FLOOD

## M. A. NELSON

CREATION
HOUSE
A STRANG COMPANY

M. A. Nelson has an amazing ability to bring life to words! The storytelling is not only articulate and insightful, but the creativity also draws you into the depth of our unique human culpabilities. Noah and his family trusted God no matter what anyone else said! Would I do the same? I couldn't put the book down! In fact, I was mad it had to end. I can't wait for more!

—REV. KIRK PETERMAN
PRESIDENT, RED OAK HEALING MINISTRY
IRVINE, CA

Wow—truly thought provoking! The author takes current trends in the secular world and extrapolates them to their ultimate conclusion. These are sharply contrasted with the godly values demonstrated by the Arcmann family. We have come frighteningly close to the conditions that required God's judgment of the world in the time of Noah.

—MICHAEL FARMER
MAJOR, USAF, RET.
PRESCOTT, AZ

*The Flood* is a warning cry of what can happen if some of the issues discussed in the book are allowed to fully develop in our current society. It is a timely, action-packed thriller that will leave you on the edge of your seat and wanting more. It will challenge you into action.

—LINDA ENGSTROM
WILDOMAR, CA

After reading M. A. Nelson's masterful coloring of the flood, I was mesmerized by its acumen and the implications on a modern society. *The Flood* is a sharp and revealing novel that everyone will truly enjoy. The comparison of events in the book against modern civilization demonstrates genuine human nature without missing a beat. As follows Genesis, so goes Revelation, where the Lord is bringing swift judgment, as in the days of Noah.

M. A. Nelson captured a very interesting perspective on modern life and prophetic happenings going on around us. *The Flood* walks us through many different lives, some clearly self absorbed and moving down destructive paths. All the while, many people go on enduring and working through these difficult times without understanding the signs of the times around them. At a certain level, we are all guilty of missing signs before us. *The Flood* has made me rethink my views on the days we live in.

—PAUL DAVI
VICE PRESIDENT, INDUSTRIAL SERVICES
PHOENIX, AZ

M. A. Nelson's novel *The Flood* is the stark and possible reality of a riveting modern-day Noah. "In the last hours, it will be like the days of Noah." The question for us today is, "Are we there yet?"

—AARON F. LOHRKE
PRESIDENT/FOUNDER
WORLDWIDE GATHERING INTERNATIONAL, INC.

I was hooked from the preface because I often ponder things from a "what if" or "how about" perspective. I have many times tried to imagine what it must have been like to experience the events of the Bible, and this story brought to life, in my mind's eye, the story of Noah. From the very first chapter it was easy to relate to Noah as an ordinary man with an extraordinary life's calling and how he was able to work his way through by having an unwavering faith in an awesome God.

—DIXON BROWN
LAGUNA HILLS, CA

Do you love a great story that keeps you on the edge of your seat, while making it impossible for you to do anything else but finish reading the story? Well, M. A. Nelson's new book *The Flood* knocked me out today. I couldn't put it down. In telling this story, she paints a picture of what our world would look like, having rejected God and become totally self focused. It is a world where personal pleasure, peace at any price, and scientific supremacy reign over truth. This book is not only a masterpiece of writing, but it also serves as a warning, calling everyone who reads it to wake up and make a difference!

—ED TANDY MCGLASSON
FORMER NFL FOOTBALL PLAYER, PASTOR, AND CONFERENCE SPEAKER
AUTHOR, *THE DIFFERENCE A FATHER MAKES* AND *BE-LOVED*

M. A. Nelson's *The Flood* takes us back to the Bible story most of us have read about since Sunday school. I can remember repeatedly watching the kids' version on video as my children were still very young. But, in this fresh and intriguing futuristic story of Noah and his family, M. A. Nelson moves us forward in a prophetic way and teaches us profound truths and principles that will prove to be a blessing and an inspiration for years to come. I loved every minute of my time reading through this amazing story. I am sure others will share a similar blessing! *The Flood* is engaging, enlightening, and a real page-turner! Thank you M. A. Nelson for listening and being obedient to that wee, small voice.

—DR. DOUGLAS DISIENA
AUTHOR OF *POSSIBILITY LIVING*

THE FLOOD by M. A. Nelson
Published by Creation House
A Strang Company
600 Rinehart Road
Lake Mary, Florida 32746
www.creationhouse.com

Unless otherwise noted, all Scripture quotations are from Holy Bible, New International Version of the Bible. Copyright © 1973, 1978, 1984, International Bible Society. Used by permission.

Design Director: Bill Johnson

Cover Designer: Amanda Potter

Library of Congress Control Number: 2008912227
International Standard Book Number: 978-1-59979-606-2

First Edition

09 10 11 12 13 — 987654321
Printed in the United States of America

*This book is dedicated to my sweetheart, best friend, and late husband, Jim. Heaven danced the day you arrived!*

# PREFACE

HAVE YOU EVER played the "What If" game? Children of all ages can entertain themselves for hours by letting their imaginations run wild with the simple premise of "What If." Little children ask themselves, "What if Mommy and Daddy get me that cute little puppy for Christmas? What will I name him? Where will he sleep?" Teenagers sit in class daydreaming: "What if I ask that girl who sits next to me in biology to go out on a date? What will we talk about?" Even as adults, we sometimes indulge ourselves with a little brain vacation and wander through the "Land of What If." Each new flight of fancy allows us to produce an amazing new universe...a stage upon which we become the valiant actors in some new adventure. How we come to cherish these creative little interludes!

Young married couples share quiet moments together asking themselves, "What if we have a son? Will he grow up to be President of the United States? What if he decides to go to some distant country to become a missionary? What will our family look like in twenty years?"

Often this harmless little mental excursion provides us with emotional distance from some obstacle with which we are struggling. It allows us to see our present situation from a clearer perspective. Sometimes God even shines His divine light upon these private musings to allow us to glimpse the possibilities of what our lives can be when we give our hearts uncompromisingly to His will and His service. I think it's possible that God uses these "What If" moments to provide us with the opportunity to step into the circumstances of many biblical stories and to walk in the footsteps of their characters so we might better understand what a profound effect their obedience to God must have had on their lives.

My attempt with this book is to transport you into the life of Noah and his family as his world is disrupted by God's plan for humanity. We can often find comfort by distancing ourselves from much of what we read in the Old and New Testaments and remaining in the position of intellectual observers. We hear sermons preached on events of such epic proportions as the Flood with such regularity—and delivered with such serenity, in the manner of a dispassionate overview—that we can unconsciously convince ourselves we are merely studying history. Our perspective becomes so lofty that it is virtually impossible to understand, let alone empathize with, the human beings about whom we are reading in these texts. In fact, that's what the stories of the Bible become to us: pages of historical fact that can't be relevant today. We think that the circumstances were different "in those days." *That sort of thing could never happen nowadays, not to me or to my family.* And we allow an intellectual wall to be built, which separates us from relationship with a living, loving God who can and will touch our lives today if we would only pull down the walls that separate us.

Perhaps we could better understand what happened during the days surrounding the Flood if we allowed ourselves to momentarily suspend whatever knowledge we may have of the chronology of the Bible to consider this question: "What if the Flood didn't occur during the time of the Old Testament? What if God spoke to Noah today? What kind of man would he be? How would he obey God? What would his family, friends, neighbors, or business associates think if he suddenly became preoccupied with a superhuman task required of him by God? Would anyone believe him? What would he have to risk in order to obey God's commands?"

More importantly, "What if God spoke to you today? What would you do?"

So I ask you to sit back and suspend your knowledge of Bible history for a moment and enter into the realm of "What If."

Let's escape our Sunday School songs of Noah and the ark. Let's escape the pictures of a cute little boat with cute little animals marching in two by two with smiles on their faces. Let's take a journey together and see if we can catch a glimpse of what it would really be like if the Flood were to happen in the not-too-distant future.

THE FLOOD

The very depths were convulsed.
The clouds poured down water,
The skies resounded with thunder;
Your arrows flashed back and forth.
Your thunder was heard in the whirlwind,
Your lightning lit up the world;
The earth trembled and quaked.

—PSALM 77:16–18

D ON'T KEEP THROWING the worms overboard, Jake." Shem glared at his youngest brother with a look that indicated his obvious disapproval of Jake's immature behavior. After all, this was a day of fishing with Dad and that was serious stuff.

"But the fish are hungry and I just want to feed some of them," replied Jake with a stubborn pout of his lower lip. Noah watched the scene with a smile as he showed Ham how to tie on his lure so the knot wouldn't come undone again. Oh how he loved these outings with his sons in their little twenty-foot outboard.

Noah chose this boat because it was perfect for fishing and Sara would feel safe when he and the boys traveled some distance to chase the elusive yellowtail or some other fish that happened along the California coast. Sometimes they would get so carried away with fishing that they would go out a little farther than planned, but their boat was equipped with all the modern technology available. The "toys" on board included a state-of-the-art depth finder, global positioning satellite equipment, and fish locators so precise they almost could print out the species one was sailing over. Of course, the boys were fascinated by all the gadgets and by how everything worked.

Sometimes Noah would daydream while they were fishing. He could envision these trips becoming a great family tradition passed down to his grandsons. What a joy it would be to have three generations of Arcmanns out on the ocean together, sharing stories, sandwiches, and laughter. They might even need a bigger boat to hold that many rowdy youngsters. Everything seemed right with the world at that moment.

*It just doesn't get any better than this.* Noah looked out over the ocean towards the horizon. He couldn't help but notice how unusually flat and glass-like the water's surface was this morning. It was still. Very still. The sun was shining and there wasn't a cloud in the sky.

He turned his attention back to tying Ham's lure on his line. It was funny, though, no matter what they did today, they just couldn't seem to get a bite. That wasn't normal. They were all pretty good fishermen, except, of course, little Jake. But nothing they tried today seemed to work. Noah's mind drifted to the old saying, "There's no such thing as a bad day of fishing!"

His thoughts were interrupted by Ham pointing off the bow, "Look, Dad. Look at that school of fish breaking the surface over there."

Noah watched as hundreds of small, silvery fish frantically broke the surface as though they were being chased by a larger fish. "Cast over there," he shouted to the boys. "Maybe we can hook whatever's chasing them."

Before he got the last words out, both boys were casting over in the direction of the fleeing fish, just behind what appeared to be the back of the school. Although his boys truly loved one another, there was still a fierce competitive streak that ran through them, no matter what they were doing. Fishing was no exception. Both Ham and Shem were intent on being the first to catch a fish today. They each wanted to have the cherished honor of having caught the biggest and the most.

Jake pulled on his Dad's fishing vest, "Daddy! Daddy, look."

"Just a minute, son, we're trying to find at least one fish out here that hasn't had his lunch yet."

"But Daddy," Jake insisted, "There's big fish over there. Lots of them."

Noah turned to see what his youngest son was pointing at. He couldn't believe his eyes. Another school of fish was breaking water like the previous school. But these were considerably larger than the anchovies now running off the bow of the boat. Shem and Ham both caught sight of the activity, and, in a flash, they were casting in the direction of the scattering school of fish around them. Both were squealing with delight at the prospect of catching one of these trophies.

Noah watched his older sons work up a sweat trying to be the first with a fish on the line. Jake clapped his chubby little hands together cheering them on. Noah noticed a small dark cloud, about the size of a man's fist, moving in from off shore. For some reason he couldn't take his eyes off this cloud. The cloud appeared strange, but in a way he could not quite understand. This bizarre formation moved toward them at an alarming speed, despite the fact that there was no evidence of any wind. The ocean was glassy all around them, except where the crazed fish were jumping, making the water boil and foam.

He continued to stare at this cloud, which slowed and hovered over the water. Slowly it spread out in a long, thin, black line parallel to the shore. The more elongated it became, the more it grew in density and depth, billowing and rolling in place, churning puffs of purple, indigo, and black as it began to stretch across the horizon. The sky began to darken all around them. Was it his imagination or was this cloud actually descending to touch the surface of the water?

Noah had been out on the ocean ever since he was a lad, just like his sons. He had grown up on the water. He knew that storms could sometimes materialize very quickly, so he was always careful to check weather reports before going out. There had been nothing in the weather reports for this area. He didn't want to take chances, especially since they were several miles farther out than normal. He'd thought it would be safe enough on such a sunny day and with such flat water.

Something inside was telling him that this was serious but he didn't want to alarm his boys. *Time to head for shore and fast.* As he started up the motor, he told the boys to reel in their lines and prepare everything in case it started to rain. The boys busied themselves checking their life vests, making sure Jake was secured in his jacket, and stowing all the gear in the proper compartments. Noah turned back to check on this eerie storm cloud. His heart stopped. He rubbed his eyes and tried to refocus on the horizon again. *I must be imagining things.* The cloud had touched down along the entire horizon and was sucking the ocean up into itself, creating a growing wall of water reaching skyward.

"This is impossible," Noah said in amazement. "I've seen water-spouts form over the ocean when a severe storm whips them up from the surface. But they are generally like small twisters and dissipate shortly. This is all wrong." He rubbed his eyes. "This doesn't look anything like a waterspout. This looks like a tidal wave. But it can't be. They're not formed like this."

A wall of water was definitely forming from this unholy union of the black cloud and the ocean. Just then the cloud seemed to let go of the water and started moving rapidly towards shore. The wave that it formed traveled independently of the cloud and rushed towards them. It stretched across the entire horizon, or at least where the horizon had been before this nightmare began. The wave, awesome and terrifying at the same time, arched towards the heavens to nearly one hundred feet.

Noah was wrenched back to reality. The boat, caught in a swell, arched skyward and fell abruptly. The boys screamed in unison as water cascaded over the sides threatening to swamp them if they didn't move quickly. Noah fought the fear tightening his throat. He jammed the engine to full throttle and headed for shore. Dark, ominous clouds billowed overhead. Seagulls flew frantically in every direction, squawking a warning. Noah grasped the wheel with one hand as he motioned his boys close to him with the other. A series of increasingly larger and fiercer waves battered their boat. They couldn't see land in any direction because of the clouds blocking the sunlight.

"Daddy! Daddy, where are we?" Jake sobbed as he wrapped his arms around Noah's leg and held tight. "What's happening, Daddy? We want to go home, Daddy!"

Noah sensed something horrendous building. His grip on the steering wheel tightened, as did the growing knot in his stomach. Every muscle in his body was constricting, ready to fight for survival. Noah couldn't even hear his sons over the incredible noise generated by this rushing mountain of salt water. It started with a rhythmic pounding that jolted his entire body and filled his eardrums to bursting. This monstrous aberration of the ocean approached at an incredible speed and with such a deafening noise that it would have drowned out the loudest jet engines.

A part of Noah wanted to imagine this as some mythological sea monster coming up from its ancient lair miles beneath the ocean. He desperately wanted to believe that it would all disappear as he regained his senses. His imagination was now playing tricks on him. Maybe they had mistakenly drifted above the nose of a highly secret nuclear submarine whose existence was unknown to the United States or its allies; some horrific weapon of destruction that was about to break the surface and crush them with its enormous weight, leaving scarcely a remnant for anyone to identify. His heart beat so loudly in his ears it was almost as loud as the fearsome roar approaching. Cold water splashed over the boat, rocking him back to this horrible reality.

"Grab that bucket, Shem, and give the other bucket to Ham," he shouted above the deafening roar. "Start bailing, boys!"

He could tell by the look of terror on their faces that they were struggling to comprehend the impending disaster. He turned to see the monster wave closing the distance at frightening speed. The ocean supernaturally rose to form this curved wall almost a hundred feet high, which now sped directly toward their tiny boat at a heart-stopping rate. A boiling wall of salt water was building in speed and height simultaneously as Noah and the boys watched, paralyzed with terror. There was no escape. They could never reach land in time. The sound of thunder was drowning them as if it were the water itself pounding the life out of them. Noah pressed his hands tightly over his ears, but it still wasn't enough to drown out the sound, permeating his entire being. And yet in it all, there was a familiar sound. The sound of something recognizable deep within his soul.

# CHAPTER TWO

NOAH. NOAH. NOAH." He was sure he had heard his name being called repeatedly above the roar. Or was he simply going mad in this moment? He desperately tried to call out the name of Jesus. He pleaded with God to come rescue him and his little family from this impending disaster. He felt that his vocal chords were going to explode from trying to shout with every ounce of breath.

Noah lay perfectly still. A deathly quiet enveloped him, pierced only by the beating of his heart. He was soaked and dared not open his eyes. As he ran his tongue over his lips, he tasted salt. He made a quick inventory of his body, checking for any sign of broken bones. He slowly opened his eyes. It was dark, except for the warm golden glow of the nightlight in the adjoining bathroom. Noah bolted upright in his bed. His body, drenched in sweat, shook.

He couldn't breathe. This nightmare was so real. He could smell the ocean air.

He eased his six-foot-plus frame out of the bed he shared with his wife, Sara. *It's a good thing that she is such a sound sleeper.* He didn't want to trouble her with these nightmares he'd been having. Lately, they had been coming more frequently and with greater intensity of detail. At first, they were merely scattered thoughts, like small film clips running across the screen in his mind. There was no context, no beginning, middle, or end. They were just random mental snapshots, but full color with surround sound. He felt like he was being transported into his own private movie studio, but no one had given him the script.

Nothing about the dreams made much sense, which was why he didn't want to bother Sara with the details. She was always more methodical and less emotional in her approach to her studies. She liked to gather all the pertinent information and arrange it into logical groupings before even beginning to formulate a theory. Noah had more of the hands-on approach. He liked to hypothesize while in the process of accumulating facts, being ever vigilant to make theoretical adjustments as new facts presented themselves. But this just wasn't an ordinary scientific puzzle that needed to be solved. Deep within him, Noah could feel something strange welling up in his spirit, and he didn't have a clue as to what was approaching.

As he did so often in his career when stumped with any research project problem, he got up quietly, pulled on a pair of comfortable old sweats, and padded barefoot out to the kitchen to fix a pot of his favorite personal blend of rich, bold Columbia coffee with a touch of espresso bean mixed in. The aroma of freshly brewing coffee helped him shake the cobwebs and get his mind clicking again.

This morning, he decided to spend his devotional time with the Lord in the comfort of the family room instead of his customary well-worn leather chair in his study and research lab. His lab was in a modest building at the easternmost end of their property. It had originally been a small barn, and Sara had suggested that with a little creativity it would make a wonderful research lab that they could easily share without even bumping into one another. He didn't have quite the imagination for that sort of thing but had every confidence in Sara's ability to take a thought and make it materialize into the real thing. And she kept her word. She transformed the run-down old home for horses into a high-tech lab. She managed to design a floor plan that combined the best in cutting-edge equipment in both their fields of research with secluded individual areas for private contemplation. Both private study areas reflected their individual tastes and provided them with what she called "inspiration room."

Sara had integrated floor to ceiling banks of windows along both sides of the building to wash every corner in natural light. For the occasional overcast or foggy California morning, she installed a few well-placed skylights with light shades. She preferred lots of light because of her work and love of plant life. For Noah the light simply provided a feeling of life that came pouring in from the sun. It regenerated his mental, emotional, and spiritual batteries and helped him to stay fresh. He had requested that part of his study area be arranged with an overstuffed leather sofa and chair for his quiet times of meditation on the Bible. He cherished his time alone with the Lord to consult over the seemingly insurmountable problems of life and, of course, science too. If something were troubling him and he couldn't sleep at night, he could often be found sprawled out in his leather chair, coffee in one hand and Bible in the other, having a long conversation with God.

Among his daily prayers was one of thanks to God for providing him with such a perfect life's mate in Sara. She complimented him in every way that God intended, as if they were a puzzle, with each having the interlocking piece the other needed to make a complete picture. They constantly encouraged each other as they followed their spiritual journey through life, keeping each other's eyes focused upon finding the Lord's will in every situation. Noah could remember so many times during the boys' adolescence and throughout their teen years when he and Sara would come up against a typical and particularly difficult stage the boys were going through. Oftentimes the situation would cause Noah to be at his wit's end. He would stomp out to the lab and find Sara in her study, curled up on her favorite floral sofa with her eyes closed and her Bible open on her lap listening to one of her favorite CDs. Noah would just stand for a few minutes quietly watching her. Sara always seemed so much at peace with the Lord in those moments. Sometimes she would open her eyes, smile, and motion for him to come join her on the sofa. They would pray together and talk and somehow, in the course of a few hours together, would feel the Lord's hand guide them through another rough spot on the parenting road.

Of course the tables would just as often be turned too. Sara was normally a very gentle, soft-spoken individual. She invariably had a kind word of encouragement for everyone around her. She loved people into the family with a hug and a smile and the occasional piece of her famous "Mile High Apple Pie." Noah had given her apple pies that nickname the first time he tasted one. They were huge and overflowed with her special blending of ripe Granny Smith and sweet McIntosh apples. With a piece of Sara's warm apple pie and an ice-cold glass of milk, everything miraculously seemed right in the world.

Sara was also a woman of strong beliefs and opinions. While it took a very long time for her fuse to burn, she could be known to exhibit a spark of temper. There was just a moment where, if you knew her well, as Noah and the boys certainly did, you would see the normal twinkle in her beautiful brown eyes replaced by a flash of fire. No one ever saw her act on her anger because she never wanted intentionally to do or say anything that would hurt someone else's feelings. Noah and the boys never pushed matters any further, either, because that flash of fire in her eyes was warning enough. At those times, when Sara came to the end of her rope in some impossible family dilemma or an insurmountable scientific glitch, she would be the one to seek refuge in the lab.

She might be struggling with some simple problem in her research that she knew had an easy answer, but she couldn't quite see it. She'd run the data over and over and still nothing. Then she'd remember something that Noah had taught her when they were first dating in college.

"Sometimes the most important thing is to know when to stop," Noah often advised.

Noah always enjoyed these quiet moments alone with his prayers and thoughts, as the daylight would break over the back fence of their home. He felt so close to the Lord at these times. He especially felt comforted when he took some perplexing scientific problem and presented it to God in his prayers. It seemed to lift the burden of the solution from his shoulders and often seemed to lift the fog from his brain and allow the answer to materialize.

He could hear someone shuffling about in the kitchen. The familiar sounds of coffee being stirred drifted into the family room. *Sara's up early today,* he thought. She wasn't much of a morning person, so she'd probably just quietly pour herself a cup of coffee and go back to their bedroom to start her morning rituals. She was a lot more coherent after she had some time to completely wake up. Noah closed his eyes, settled back into his chair, and let his thoughts turn back to his prayer journal.

He'd started this habit of writing his prayer concerns in a daily journal back in college. He knew he had a tendency to let his thoughts drift while he was trying to pray over the concerns in his life. His grandpa had encouraged him as a young boy to keep a journal of his prayer concerns, and he'd found it very useful throughout his life. Oftentimes it helped to put things down on paper in order to know what direction to pray. Sometimes it seemed that all he could do was to write a particular issue down in his journal because he didn't know what to pray anymore. This was one of those times. He was so disturbed by these recurring dreams. He felt like they might be from the Lord, but he hadn't a clue what to make of them.

"Lord, what are you trying to tell me? What do you want me to do? I just don't understand."

"Hello, Brother." The deep, raspy voice interrupted his prayer. Noah nearly jumped out of his seat, spilling what was left in the coffee cup he had precariously balanced on the arm of the chair. It took him a moment to realize whose voice had wrenched him out of his quiet meditation.

"Shem! When did you get into town?" Noah tried unsuccessfully to make it look as if he always reacted this way when his oldest son entered a room. When Shem was still living at home, he would often join Noah in the family room in the morning for devotions. Shem had started referring to his brothers and Noah as "Brother" as a term of affection for their brotherhood in the Lord. Shem drew out the word as if it had more than a few syllables. Somewhere during his travels he'd acquired a slight southern accent which endeared him to his wife Hope's Texan parents.

"Why so jumpy, Dad?" Shem grinned sheepishly. "I didn't mean to scare you. I thought for sure you heard me pouring coffee in the kitchen."

Noah hadn't been surprised by Shem like that since he was eight years old. He'd been fishing all day in the creek that flowed across the back of their property. When Noah came in from the lab that evening, Shem told him that he wanted to surprise him with the fish he'd caught. Shem was so proud that Noah couldn't wait to see what tiny, little rainbow trout he might have been lucky enough to snag. Shem took him by the hand and led him to the freezer in the garage where they kept all the extra supplies for the house.

"Close your eyes, Dad," Shem instructed. Noah followed orders and stood beside the freezer. Shem lifted the lid.

"You can look now."

Noah peered over the edge of the freezer. Shem chuckled at the expression on his Dad's face when he saw a fifty-pound frozen halibut staring back at him. Noah didn't know that his neighbor Jared had dropped by earlier in the day and asked if he could leave this halibut he'd caught on his last fishing trip in their freezer overnight. Shem just couldn't pass up an opportunity to play a little joke on Dad, and this was the best so far.

# CHAPTER THREE

D
R. BRANDON NOAH Arcmann was not your typical fifty-ish scientist. His rugged good looks and youthful energy would place him more easily on some beach chasing the next wave. He was definitely not a man fond of the stuffy and cavernous research libraries found in most prestigious universities. Noah had earned the respect and admiration of his colleagues for his research into the effects of the encroachment of civilization upon the animal kingdom and the subsequent extinction of its species.

His wife Sara, an agricultural scientist, specialized in the study of the effect of modern farming techniques as they promote or detract from the ultimate long-term productivity of the land. Her world-wide research led her to publish a book comparing ancient methods of farming used throughout the centuries by many of the so-called undeveloped cultures around the globe to the modern techno-growth and readaptation techniques being promoted by the billion-dollar chemical conglomerates. Her controversial conclusions had sparked heated arguments in both the scientific community and the Worldwide Association of Land Managers.

The WALM, as they call themselves, is a tight-knit community of farmers across the globe who have united in their efforts to become better stewards of what they consider the dwindling reserves of productive land throughout the earth. These men and women discovered they needed to take advantage of the modern methods of computer technology to communicate with each other and share whatever information may be helpful to prevent themselves and their industry from becoming extinct. As they began to communicate on a more regular basis, they discovered they had several things in common; one was that a significant number of these farmers had begun to revert back to the agricultural techniques recorded thousands of years ago in the Bible and had experienced significantly positive results.

They also discovered that the majority of them had been raised with traditional Christian family values, although they had all drifted away from the traditions of their fathers as they embraced the more enlightened spirituality of today's modern church. They were desperate for more information that would aid in reversing the destructive effects of centuries of modern technology, chemicals, pesticides, negative crop rotation, and computer land management. In their quest for a miracle discovery, they had forged an alliance of necessity with Sara Arcmann, Ph.D.

Noah and Sara's lives weren't always so global. They met while attending a mid-week Bible study in one of the freshman dorms at UCLA. They were both native Californians. He had grown up in Newport Beach and she a little further north in Malibu. They discovered they shared much in common. They both came from traditional middle-class families with deep religious beliefs. Noah's father had been the pastor of a small non-denominational church in Newport Beach before he passed away a few years after the death of his wife. Sara's family had a multi-generational Lutheran background. Sara had no remaining family as both of her parents had been killed some years before in a tragic car accident. Noah and Sara shared strong convictions about the importance of their relationship with God and a depth of faith that helped them through many emotionally and financially trying times during their early married life.

Noah and Sara married just before they started graduate school, and Sara gave birth to their three sons, Shem, Hamilton, and Japheth, shortly after. The couple's friends constantly chided them about having a taste for adventure because tackling graduate school or starting a family were both equally challenging and fearsome. But they decided they could do both, and with God's help and a lot of creative time management and teamwork, they made it through their doctorate programs and parenthood with their sense of humor intact and a love that was forged in steel.

While their graduate studies and research took them around the globe, they always considered California home and it was here where they had primarily raised their family. Although their sons never lacked for adventure through their parents' often exotic travels, Noah and Sara made sure that the boys were grounded in old-fashioned family values. They worked to instill a sense of continuity and stability in their little family that would allow their sons to grow and mature into strong individuals with equally strong convictions.

Shem, the oldest of the three, bore the closest resemblance to Noah. He was tall and had the rugged look of an outdoorsman and shared the dark, sapphire blues eyes of his Dad. Like his father, he was equally at ease on his boat off the Southern California coast fishing for yellowtail as he was in the lab poring over the latest results of a cattle cloning program in Japan. Noah had started Shem fishing when he was barely old enough to hold onto the side of their little fishing boat with one chubby hand and clutch a miniature fishing pole in the other. His love of boats, the salt air, and fishing remained with him throughout his life. When he was about six years old, Noah took him on a special outing, a father-son adventure to a local boat show held at Anaheim Stadium. They walked among the many varieties of boats, both modern and antique.

On the way home Noah asked Shem, "How did you like seeing all those beautiful boats, son?"

Shem replied gleefully, "Daddy, someday I'm going to build a huge ship, bigger than anything we saw today. And it's going to be so strong and fast that we will go all over the world and even fly as high as the mountains."

Noah laughed at his son's enthusiasm and even more at his outrageous imagination. *Boats that fly higher than mountains. Who knows what inventions will come out of the next century's technology when you have such young, fertile minds to work with?*

Ham was also tall but had more of a wiry build. He had the chestnut, curly hair and deep brown eyes of his mother. Like Sara, he was very methodical in his approach to life. While his looks would lead you to believe that he was a typical California surfer, his real joy came from working with his hands in the rich, brown, velvety soil around their home. Like his mother, he had a green thumb and an insatiable curiosity about how things could be grown more effectively and produce a higher quality of plant while preserving the integrity of the soil.

Ham was used to being teased unmercifully by his family. Whenever one of the family surprised Ham while he was working with his plants, they would always hear him quietly talking with the flowers or shrubs that he was tenderly nurturing. He believed that everything created by God had a spark of His spirit, which is what kept it in existence. All creation came from the loving, creative hand of the Almighty, and he could do nothing less than treat each precious plant with tender care while appreciating the intricacy and beauty that God had woven into every one.

Japheth was the baby of the family. They called him Jake. He was shorter than his two older brothers, stocky and very strong. He had an unruly thatch of wavy red hair and a beard to match. He could always be seen with a checked, flannel shirt straining over his muscular arms and shoulders. He didn't resemble anyone in his immediate family, but perhaps some distant lumberjack relative on his father's side could account for Jake's swarthy appearance and love of working with his hands. He was a builder, a hands-on scientist. His interests spanned both the areas of agriculture and the world of animals. Whether he was in the outback of Australia studying kangaroo habitat or deep in the Amazon jungles helping villagers discover better ways of producing crops to sustain their villages without destroying the rain forest, Jake was always in the middle of the action and up to his elbows.

Noah and Sara's sons were all strong, intelligent men of character with well-defined beliefs in the values of the Bible regarding their lives, families, and careers. They followed closely in their parents' footsteps, which was indeed a novelty in today's world. In a time of what is loosely referred to as moral tolerance and non-absolutism, their family stood out like a lightning rod. All three sons were happily married to their college sweethearts. The wives chose to set aside their immediate career pursuits in favor of assisting their husbands in establishing themselves in their individual fields of expertise. They were also the stabilizing factors in each marriage, producing a warm and loving home wherever their work took them.

Each of the brothers and their spouses wanted to raise their children and not worry about having someone else's values instead of their own instilled into their offspring. Each family had decided it was their responsibility to provide their children with the best educational environment they could possibly attain. The wives were all very close to one another and would often find themselves discussing the same concerns whenever they had the opportunity to gather for a family holiday. To many, they seemed far more like sisters than sisters-in-law. Not surprisingly they had all decided to homeschool their children when the time came. Of course, this would compliment their globetrotting lifestyles as well. But, for the moment, they were all too busy assisting their husbands in their various projects to even consider starting families just yet.

While still in college, the brothers and their soon-to-be brides were often ridiculed by their peers for making such traditional and "politically incorrect" choices in this age of technology. They had become accustomed to some of the good-humored teasing of their college friends whenever they would gather round and dream about the future, careers, and family. Graduation day was long past. Now their friends were all consumed in the corporate "Rung Race," as Shem liked to refer to the struggle up the corporate ladders. College pals soon drifted apart and the Arcmann brothers found that their colleagues in the scientific community had little tolerance for what they deemed pious or emotionally charged religious beliefs. Their world was a world dominated by scientific facts with no place for moral sentimentality.

Jake, Ham, and Shem were content to follow their convictions and were each blessed with wives who loved them and thoroughly supported them. The blessings flowing down from their choices were obvious in the life and joy that permeated their families. For the last seven years they had all been scattered across the various continents by their individual research projects, so they had little opportunity to spend any quantity of time together. But that was all about to be radically changed.

# CHAPTER FOUR

D EAD MAN CURLS at Greef Beach, Thursday after twelve
noon," screeched the sportscaster on the evening news.

They weren't calling them tidal waves or even
tsunamis anymore, not even on the evening news reports. Lately,
the monster waves had been coming with such regularity and the
scientific detection devices had now become so sophisticated, that
the newscasters were fairly accurate in their predictions.

A lot had changed in the past decades, mused Noah to himself as
he diced garlic for his famous "Pasta Prima Noah" the family loved
so much. The evening news, for one, had gradually morphed into a
television extravaganza that pushed its way into peaceful evening
rituals as gracelessly as a hippopotamus thrashing through a rose
garden. Long gone were the television icons of Walter Cronkite,
Ted Koppel, and Peter Jennings. They were now the dinosaurs of
the profession whose position and habits were relegated to dusty
history books. Their old-school type of reporting had become too
stylized and stunted for worldwide audience appeal.

According to their own published polls, global audiences
desired to be "moved" when they received information concerning
the world condition. Audiences demanded information in brief,
exciting sound bites. The pollsters were confident that the viewers
wanted to be entertained by the latest breaking news, no matter
what the content, no matter what level of violence or triviality and

they seemed to want it all delivered in the most current jargon made popular by the ever broadening influence of the monolithic entertainment industry. Of course, that had necessitated the rearing of a totally new breed of newscaster, one who would be politically correct in all aspects including a physical appeal that would rival even Hollywood's best.

Global appeal was also a paramount consideration in hiring, or more accurately, casting, whoever would sit behind the news desk. The station executives had all joined forces to maintain what they considered a uniformity of excellence in their presentation of the news. The American station executives often congratulated and rewarded themselves for elevating news delivery to a new art form; one to be envied by the rest of the world. They prided themselves, not on how accurate their information was, nor on its timeliness, not even on its ability to genuinely inform the general public on issues that seriously impacted their lives or gave them pause when they went to the ballot box. Instead they imposed a uniform code of what Noah liked to term "ethical anesthesia."

Noah often told Sara that he could imagine the discussions around huge marble-topped tables in the executive boardrooms at these network conferences in New York or Los Angeles. They weren't arguing over hard-hitting reporting of current political events across the globe; they weren't trying to out-scoop each other on the latest Oval Office scandal. They were consumed, with every bit as much fervor, in discussing what fashion trends they would emulate in their news reporters' wardrobes; what terminology was in vogue with the latest voter bloc or special interest group; what world event could best be presented in an entertaining fashion that would "report" it, while not offending *any* faction *anywhere* on the planet. News had become entertainment with the depth of an afternoon soap opera and perhaps not quite as much drama.

News broadcasters no longer referred to each other as Kaitlin, the weather person, but Kaitlin, the weather citizen. There was Mel, the sports citizen, or Steven, the national news citizen. They purposely dispensed with the ancient terms *newsman, sportsman, weather girl.* Every aspect of this was carefully scripted and the players cast to project the most hip, up-to-the-minute impression possible. Of course, this meant the audience was subjected to an ever-changing array of "actors" as they tuned in to the evening news each night. The faces changed rapidly as some newsperson's current political attitude, social standing, or bronzed good looks went quickly out of vogue to be replaced with whatever new and improved version was currently popular. After all, ratings were everything. In some circles, it was even murmured that ratings could be responsible for a great many unsavory and even criminal goings on behind the scenes in the entertainment business. "The Media Mafia" they were called by some of the old school. They were the few major moguls and their "families" that seemed to control what the world of entertainment and news packaged and promoted for public consumption. The news now had become firmly entrenched in the category of entertainment instead of historical documentation of current facts.

In fact, printed news had long since left the scene around the world. Ostensibly, it became less globally correct to sacrifice nature's resources for something as mundane as a local or national newspaper. After all, everyone who would even harbor the slightest interest in current events probably had access to one or more personal computers and was linked to one of the many telecommunication networks that offered the services of the Micro Global Access Connection or MGAC (known to net surfers as GAC).

Why waste precious natural resources on newsprint, when society had become accustomed to the quick fix that only electronic communication could provide? If anyone still wanted to experience the nostalgia of reading, there were a plethora of portable electronic reading devices on the market, which gave one the illusion of reading a book without the bulky paper and binding. The newspaper industry did not give up without a fight, however. There were many of what were labeled right-wing conservatives that wanted to preserve this industry, if for no other reason than to maintain its place in history or simply for nostalgia. Perhaps they enjoyed exercising their reading skills and imagination and felt more accustomed to digesting information through the written word than the often hypnotizing effects of visual news quips on TV. Whatever their reasons, they protested long and loud, but ultimately to no avail.

Rumors surfaced periodically of some "right wing" or "left wing" underground newsletter being clandestinely circulated throughout the United States. The powers that be didn't seem concerned about these little niche "bulletins" having any devastating effects. Besides, the governments around the globe felt these small, under-financed, and self-righteous publications were primarily directed to the "Christian" element. The Christians certainly had tried to become more vocal some years back, especially when it came to preserving fundamental rights as assigned to the people by God and the Constitution. But world powers felt Christians were becoming less of a threat as the media constantly undermined their credibility with inflammatory news quips focused only on fanatical groups rather than on what had once been considered mainstream Christians.

Religion had become a very powerful tool. But the religion of today was a far cry from what the American founding fathers considered worship of the "one true God." Today's religion was a religion of self-improvement that was sponsored and supported by every world government on the earth. Each country had a slightly different approach but the goals were all becoming very similar. Religion pointed you to a universal "Higher Source" which would ultimately help perfect your time here on earth. Religion was a person's inner journey to self-fulfillment. Every government on the planet had a self-serving interest in spreading the international religion of self-worth and inner peace. The ultimate goal of every religion was now world peace. The best way to achieve this lofty goal was to make sure that the indoctrination began in the schools so students could aspire to "be all that they could be" and that was to be a "good global citizen." A good global citizen was, of course, a citizen whose primary ambition was to support the team in whatever was best for the majority. Their life was focused on promoting a global, earth consciousness.

"Ouch!" Noah threw down the paring knife.

He knew better than to slice and dice while letting his thoughts wander. Sara always told him that she could sense a rise in his blood pressure every time a conversation strayed in this direction. Well, there was certainly nothing he could do about any of it. He just added his concerns to his ever-expanding prayer journal under the heading "World Concerns." Whatever had distracted him to thinking about all this anyway?

*Oh, yes.* The newscaster had reported on the "Dead Man Curls." The curls concerned Noah for several reasons. These tidal waves had been coming more frequently in the last year and with some predictability. From a scientific perspective, they were enormously fascinating and, no doubt, were the harbingers of some monumental shift in world weather patterns as well as potentially significant geologic shifts in the tectonic plates worldwide. His instincts kept sounding an alarm that he couldn't ignore.

There was also the issue of those recurring dreams he'd been having. He wasn't sure if they were dreams or nightmares, but he sensed there was a message unfolding in them and he couldn't quite grasp it yet. He was convinced the dreams and these news bites were somehow connected. *But how?* He decided to add this to his prayer journal, asking the Lord to give him insight into what the purpose of these dreams might be for him and his family. But, during his prayers lately, he seemed to be doing all the talking. Noah assumed God was listening, albeit silently, and didn't seem in any hurry to respond.

Another aspect of the "Dead Man Curls" reports always sent shivers down his spine. This pop nickname for devastating waves originated from young people around the world. They tagged the tidal waves with that moniker because that was how they regarded the kids who chose to follow them around the globe. They were today's version of surfers, but surfers who had no desire to achieve anything lasting in this world. Their claim to fame would be making some list of hundreds of names of those foolish enough to have tried to tame nature at full force. If the waves won, they were "Dead Men."

It pained him to see that so much of today's youth had long since given up on a bright and promising future. They had become so anesthetized by a continual diet of television fantasy, computer relationships, sexual freedom, and drug use that they were becoming zombies. They desperately ached to feel alive again. They wanted to *feel* something, anything, and flirting with almost certain death by attempting to ride the tidal wave curls was their new drug of choice and their ticket from obscurity to their fifteen minutes of fame. It didn't really matter if they lived or died in the attempt. It was all about the rush!

It infuriated Noah and Sara that there was, in fact, a small and infamous band of young men and women who traveled around the globe in search of the meanest tidal wave yet. They were known simply as "The Riders." Somehow, despite incredible odds against their survival for any length of time in this vocation, they continued to avoid the inevitable, icy grasp of death. Their exploits were constantly splashed across TV screens after another brutal display of nature's wrath against some unsuspecting shoreline. They would appear before the cameras taunting other teens and young people to "Give it a try." They strutted before the eyes of the world and issued these brutish challenges at every opportunity. Each time they survived, they recruited more disillusioned youth to follow them and embrace almost certain death. Sara often expressed her concern at seeing these spectacles on the evening news with increased frequency.

She'd said to Noah on more than one occasion, "Look into their eyes, Noah. What do you see?"

Noah peered intently at the youthful faces on the screen. "Nothing. Absolutely nothing. It's like their eyes are vacant."

"But there's something more than that, Noah. It's as if some*one*, or some*thing* was staring back at you from behind their eyes; something very, very evil. And then it just disappears in a flash."

Noah remembered that conversation each time these stories were televised. He began to pay closer attention and felt he could see it too. It frightened him more than he would like to admit.

Sara came into the kitchen soaking wet from a swim before dinner. She lightly toweled her luxurious chestnut mane of hair. Looking at her silhouetted against the brilliant colors of the sunset still took away Noah's breath. Noah was beginning to feel a part of the fifty-something generation and was becoming a bit more concerned about the few extra inches creeping up around his athletic build. Not Sara. She was special. They were only a few years apart in age, but even after three children she seemed more beautiful and energetic than when they first met as youngsters. She caught him staring at her and it made her blush.

"What's on the menu, chef?" She playfully reached around him, kissed him on the cheek, and stole a few carrot slices from the counter in front of him. "Do I have time for a quick shower and change of clothes before dinner?"

"You'll spoil my incredibly precise measurements for this special recipe if you keep that up," Noah teased.

"Since when did you start measuring anything when it comes to cooking, Monsieur Chef?"

They liked to tease each other with the running joke about their different methods of cooking. Noah preferred the unrestrained creativity of using a pinch of this and a handful of that, and ultimately smelling and tasting a creation into perfection. Sara felt more secure following precise directions from any one of her dozens of cookbooks or handwritten recipes. But they both enjoyed the peacefulness of coming together in the kitchen after a hard day's work and preparing something delicious together while discussing the events of the day. The tradition had begun when the children were in diapers. Their sons continued the tradition with their own wives.

"Take your time, sweetie. There's no rush tonight. This can simmer for a while until you get done with your shower."

Sara stole a few slices of the artichoke hearts Noah was chopping up before he placed all the ingredients into his famous sauce. She scampered off for a long, leisurely shower before he could warn her about spoiling her appetite.

# CHAPTER FIVE

A NEW 'TEEN EXPRESS' just opened today in the beautiful suburb of Placid Valley. More than a thousand teens are expected here tonight for the grand opening. Of course, the prospect of experiencing the new digital virtual sound machine and the possibility of winning a brand new Venom V-8 roadster may have something to do with this great turn out."

Rionne, the newest, perky entertainment commentator on the six o'clock news was all smiles as she stood before an animated crowd of youngsters circling the block for the opportunity to be the first ones into this newest teen club. Teen Express clubs were springing up all across the globe, primarily in larger metropolitan areas in the beginning; but now they were seen even in such sleepy little suburbs as Placid Valley. Years ago, when these clubs first came on the scene, constant protests from local Christian groups were held at each place. Despite protests from various religious groups that were active at that time, the clubs continued to grow in popularity.

They were just the latest perversion served up to the youth of today in the name of "tolerant" and "pro-choice" politicians. These two terms had become the anthem of liberal, global-minded citizens of the world. The Teen Express Clubs had first gained popularity over a decade ago when Congress passed a bill officially allowing school-wide distribution of contraceptive devices to children starting in middle school. This bill also made it possible for teenage girls to have an abortion without parental consent. An addendum to the bill made it legal to expand the sex education classes to include a wide variety of related topics thought to be informative and life expanding. These decisions were heralded by the press, as well as by the politicians, as thoroughly patriotic because they felt that such legislation was finally championing long neglected children's rights.

Popular political opinion polls indicated the world had been turning a deaf ear to one of the largest minorities in existence: children and their right to freedom of choice, freedom of information, and freedom of self-actualization. After all, the retail markets had recognized this group as one of the largest spending segments of society years ago. Women's rights activists even joined the bandwagon to promote children's rights as an extension of their own platform of pro-choice. The term pro-choice had initially referred only to an adult woman's choice regarding whether or not to abort her unborn child. Thanks to the insistence of powerful lobbying groups, it had now mutated into the children's choice to explore their sexuality uninhibited by any of the conventional standards or morals that had been the benchmark of American democracy since the founding fathers set foot on this continent.

Media coverage had exploded with anti-conservative, right-wing fundamentalist marches in front of Capitol Hill, in front of the White House, in front of every state capitol building across the nation. Every time the issue surfaced, the well-meaning Christian activists were portrayed as wild-eyed Neanderthals. They were accused of being bent on turning civilization back a century and relegating sex to some fantasy, pristine state of mind that the world now found to be suffocating the natural growth and expression of upcoming generations. Pro-choice demonstrators and lobbyists were producing plentiful, but often dubious, research to support their position. Their research purported to show that children raised in such a stifling atmosphere as described in the Bible were potentially prone to anti-social behavior as adults and rarely succeeded in the fast-paced, culturally blended society of today.

The political puppets preached from the podiums of Congress that people must have tolerance for all walks of life and for freedom of sexual expression. And they preached with a fervor that was matched only by the fervor found in the country's pulpits on Sundays as churchgoers across the nation desperately tried to find a way to shield their children from impending doom. Unfortunately, publicity and peer pressure, not to mention the obvious availability of sexually explicit materials to teenagers on campus, proved more than the church was able to counteract. Perhaps there were just too many church leaders whose own beliefs had softened throughout the years. The gospel of tolerance found its way into church after church with such enthusiastic acceptance that people soon ceased to question its Biblical authenticity. After all, once the Christians accepted peace and tolerance at all costs, they began to reap favor with the media and government.

There were, of course, small pockets of fundamentalist believers who tried to hold fast to the Word of God. They were quickly absorbed into the machinery of survival in the modern world. After all, it was not healthy to hold on to archaic views that did nothing in the past but fuel world wars. Wasn't the Bible really all about "peace and love" anyway? If people truly understood the concept of collective consciousness awareness, as taught in every classroom from kindergarten on up, they would see that peace and love was what people needed to live in harmony.

The frosting on an otherwise disgusting cake came when Nash Brookline, millionaire Senator from Massachusetts, pioneered the first Teen Express Club in Boston. Legislation had long since been passed that blurred the lines concerning conflict of interest when it involved members of Congress in partnership with private business.

Nash saw the financial bonanza on the horizon if he could popularize this notion of a club where teens could "express" themselves and experiment sexually in a "controlled and safe" environment of their peers.

Nash had thought of just about every angle. The clubs were "Membership Only" with strict requirements regarding medical history, psychological profiling, and family financial records. These clubs were available to teenagers only, and the rules were strictly enforced. Entrance was granted only after a hand scan at the door. When the teens were accepted to the clubs, they were given a small tattoo on their hand encrypted with all their relevant information. This way they could travel to any city where there was a Teen Express Club and enter by having their hand scanned at the door.

Once inside, teens were introduced to a sexual playground where they could be free to indulge in sex with anyone of their choosing, at any time, provided the potential partners were willing. Of course, some just came to observe, and it allowed them to still feel like they were part of the "in crowd." The hand tattoos were a badge of sophistication in the teen community and the younger children would look with envy upon their older siblings as they proudly sported the "TE" in the inverted triangle on the palms of their hands.

Parents even encouraged children to join these clubs, just for the status of being seen as progressive, cutting-edge parents. Some parents were relieved at not having to shoulder the responsibility of teaching their children the consequences of sexual activity apart from the benefits of marriage. Few seemed inclined to consider the biblical perspective regarding this most precious and sacred act between a man and a woman.

Nash Brookline was fast becoming the patron saint of the next generation of voters as well as their parents. His benevolent contribution of a small portion of the expansive revenues generated by the growing number of clubs to local charities and hospitals focused on caring for children of all ages endeared him to an even greater voting demographic. More than one Christian group had speculated on his motives being broader than mere financial gain. No one dared vocalize his or her concerns anymore. Each club opening provided enough free publicity opportunities to make even a veteran politician jealous. Nash had enviably been the first to manufacture such a fertile political field to plow. Cameras often could catch Senator Brookline surrounded by ecstatic teenagers and equal numbers of parents who wanted their neighbors to see just how progressive their life philosophy had become. Invariably the camera would zoom in for the requisite close up of Nash shaking some proud parent's hand while smiling victoriously into millions of homes around the world.

Each time Noah saw Brookline's face on the news he shuddered involuntarily. He couldn't quite put his finger on it, but it was somehow familiar in a sinister, cold way. There was something just behind Nash's polished and surgically enhanced appearance, something in his eyes. *He'd seen that look before, but where?*

Unfortunately, this phenomenon of Teen Express was spreading across the country and the world like a grass fire raging out of control and consuming every obstacle in its path. Noah often pondered just exactly what was breathing life into this monster at such a fevered pace. He was terrified of the answer.

# CHAPTER SIX

NOAH SHUDDERED INVOLUNTARILY. He was soaked and chilled to the bone. He couldn't catch his breath. The atmosphere surrounding him turned into liquid and he was a drowning man going down for the third time.

"Where am I? I've got to find shelter! Where's Sara? Where are the boys?"

An ear-shattering noise forced him to stumble and fall face forward into the mud and rocks. Lightning flashed across a frozen gray sky. But this noise wasn't from above; it penetrated his whole body. The earth's surface was groaning in excruciating pain. Noah struggled to regain his balance. *What caused the ground to suddenly lurch so violently beneath his feet?*

Rivers of mud streamed past him. The mud had unusual qualities that he'd never observed before. In the flat light, punctuated periodically by a shard of lightning, he glimpsed what appeared to be golden or silver particles floating by in the liquefied dirt. Great globs of this slimy substance caked on his face, hands, and clothes, making it difficult even to walk. He managed to regain his footing, and pressed forward. He wasn't sure in what direction he should travel, but he was certainly being drawn by something greater than self-preservation. As he continued to try to make his way further across the fields, he could see evidence of prior small eruptions in the earth's surface, similar to what one might see after an earthquake. These appeared different. They were like miniature volcanoes, but they oozed water. The volume of water erupting all around him kept increasing at an alarming rate.

He stooped down to examine one of the mounds of bubbling water more closely. He picked up a handful of the newly formed mud as it ran down the sides. Something sparkled and caught the light as another lightning bolt scissored across the sky. He grabbed where he saw the light sparkle. He expected his hand to close on soft mud. Instead, something hard lay in the palm of his hand. He opened it and wiped away the slimy reddish brown earth to reveal a raw diamond glittering back at him. He dropped the precious jewel in astonishment.

"How can this be happening?"

His mind ran through all the scientifically plausible explanations for what he was observing. But nothing in his years of study prepared him for the conclusions. He heard a heart-wrenching scream somewhere in the distance. He jumped to his feet, his heart racing and his legs pounding beneath him in a life and death race for safety.

"Where are you, Lord? Where are you?"

"I'm right here, sweetheart." Sara's voice brought him out of the dream. "You must have fallen asleep during the news. I didn't think I took that long to bathe." Sara bent down and gave Noah a peck on the forehead. "Noah, you're soaked. Are you feeling all right?"

"Just a bad dream, I guess, honey." He didn't want to reveal the details of this latest dream to Sara right now. He needed time to process what all this meant. He made a mental note to add these curious and frightening dreams to his prayer list the next time he had a long talk with God. Maybe it was time to ask Him what was happening.

# CHAPTER SEVEN

NOAH SORTED THROUGH the mail over a steaming cup of French Vanilla coffee. He came to the large, official-looking envelope from the Department of Global Ecological Management. They had been pursuing Noah and Sara to assume the roles of Chief Administrators for their latest and most controversial experiment. International representatives from around the world had been meeting with GEM for a number of years now trying to develop innovative methods of preventing or at least providing some damage control to some quickly diminishing species of plants and animals across the globe. Population infringement upon Amazon rain forests, African savannahs, and even snow-covered tundra was escalating at an incredible rate worldwide. Valuable and irretrievable natural resources were being lost at a vicious pace. Species of plants and animals were disappearing off the globe with no hope of retrieval and no substitutes in sight. Unless God suddenly decided to overlook the pitiful stewardship job that civilization had done over what He created and bless the globe with entirely new species on every continent, some sort of solution was needed to at least temporarily stop this catastrophe.

GEM had been involved in studies regarding the viability of interbreeding species of plants and animals for many years. Most of their research had been done under careful security because during the early years of the projects the citizenry was still very concerned about the possibility of "Big Brother" manipulating genes or cloning prospects and developing species that would become aberrations of God's perfect plan. Protestors marched nearly every week around one of the many GEM research centers around the globe. As is often the case with unproven scientific techniques, disgruntled former employees leaked out bits of unrelated information to the press and the media would devour it like piranha.

The most outspoken of these protest groups was Concerned Christians For Creation. Its members were vocal about the heinous possibilities of tampering with the environment and fervently believed God had a plan for everything and if all species of plant and animal life slowly disappeared from the earth, it would merely be a winding down of this present darkness and the beginning of the new Zion. Unfortunately they also believed God would use an interplanetary traveler to visit earth who would bring with him the new plant and animal life forms needed to start Eden again.

The news media, of course, had a field day with all this. While most Christians were content to remain safely at home and pray for whatever supposed atrocities might be carried out at these facilities, the press identified the Concerned Christians For Creation with mainline believers and made genuine protest first unbelievable and soon nonexistent. The climate of tolerance once again reared its ugly head and scientific progress took precedence over moral environmental responsibility.

Biosphere Five was going to be the ultimate in Global Resource Management. This was not only going to bring all the world's plant and animal resources under close scrutiny but it was going to be the glue that would cement President Hyland Wells' position as the next candidate for Global First Citizen. He would be the first U.S. President to accomplish the daunting task of negotiating with the world rulers for donations of their dwindling and almost extinct plant and animal species to the Biosphere Five Project.

Previous Global First Citizens had tried ardently to convince many of the nations struggling for their survival to partner in this project, but no one had been able to exert the required pressure as effectively as President Wells. He and his good friend, Senator Brookline had personally traveled to each nation that entertained even the slightest reservation about the success of this project and convinced them of its value. Coincidently, wherever the President and Senator traveled together to promote Biosphere Five, a Teen Express Club would open soon thereafter. Centuries old cultural taboos would seemingly vanish in a mist of progressive camaraderie.

Noah watched intently as the President and Senator returned home from their last trip to the glorious applause of hundreds of reporters on the White House lawn. This time Sara didn't even need to comment. President Wells and Senator Brookline held up their joined hands in a sign of victory for the media. They both flashed strikingly identical smiles. The cameras zoomed in for a close-up, and Sara and Noah both noticed that same cold, sinister glint that flashed from behind their eyes as they smiled into the lens. It was frozen for an instant and then vanished. Noah and Sara shivered simultaneously.

# CHAPTER EIGHT

W HAT TIME IS it?" shouted the announcer as he skill-fully worked the audience into a frenzy.

"It's time to…let your mind roam. Let your mind roam."

The chant rose from the frantic audience and increased in volume until it achieved an almost hypnotic primal rhythm. Most of the audience was already on its feet, arms in the air, swaying in unison as if under the powerful direction of some unseen conductor.

The familiar chant was raised every day at the taping of the *Romie Rogers Show*. Millions of viewers around the globe tuned in for their daily dose. To some, it was their drug of choice. They could indulge in the vicarious criticism of the guests; the boldest of the viewing audience could even call in via satellite link to add their judgment or condemnation of the "guest du jour." Perhaps the term criticism is too mild when relating to what was possible during one of Romie's live shows. The *Romie Rogers Show* possessed the enviable reputation of having the greatest number of guests leave the stage in tears or on the verge of a breakdown. The audience loved this opportunity to verbally brutalize whoever happened to be unlucky or unwitting enough to be a guest on this show.

The show cloaked itself in contradiction as well as controversy.

The host, Ms. Romie Rogers, seemed genuine and innocent. She had the familiar Hollywood blonde, green-eyed, surgically enhanced appearance that viewers had come to expect in talk show hosts. Yet her mannerisms, as well as her appearance, were annoyingly deceptive. In fact, her Southern manners always managed to endear her to the audience and her guests. In the industry she was known as "Southern Comfort."

"Let your mind roam. Let your mind roam."

Romie inhaled the sounds drifting into her elaborate dressing room over the discreetly mounted speaker. The sound of the audience moving together as of one mind and body were intoxicating to her. She privately referred to "The Chant" as her real theme song. After all, this was what truly got her creative juices flowing.

She sat staring into her pyramid-shaped mirror. Reaching out, she ran her long, perfectly-manicured nails along the rose etched into the lower right-hand corner. The mirror was tinted a light rose color. Romie felt it enhanced her complexion as she added her normal, last-minute personal touches to her impeccable makeup. Everything in her dressing room had an eerie rose glow about it. She felt it produced the proper changes in her aura that allowed her inner power to balance with her environment.

That's what made the rose on her mirror stand out from the rest of the room. It was the color and texture of rich, black velvet. The leaves were an iridescent emerald green that glowed even in this artificial light. More than one reporter or guest in Romie's dressing room commented on one particular detail of this magnificent rose etching. Their eyes were always drawn to the golden thorns protruding from the stem of this rose. They mesmerized the observer. The entire image had a most disconcerting and provocative effect, yet no one could avert their eyes.

Romie felt deep within her that the black rose embodied her

essence. She had created her persona very carefully. She had spent many years studying at the feet of the most well known yogi in the world, Maharishi Mondhi. After six years of intense study, she had obtained her personal spirit guide and learned how to communicate with him. Under Mondhi's expert guidance, she had gone into the eleventh trance, an altered state of consciousness that very few individuals ever achieved. Here, she divested herself of the inferior persona with which she had been born and clothed herself in her true nature. That was where Romie Rogers was born.

There had always been rumors flying through the entertainment industry about her real identity and her childhood, but the entertainment industry thrived on rumors. She didn't seem to exist before she became Romie. And in her own heart she had become convinced, with the ever-present assurance of her spirit guide, that she never had existed before on this plane.

Unknown even to her closest associates, she had come from a very common Midwestern family. She was just an ordinary young girl from a small farming community. No one particularly noticed her in school. Her grades were average, her mousy brown hair, brown eyes, and thick glasses brought her little attention from the boys. After her graduation from high school, she moved to Los Angeles to attend a Junior College. She thought that she might want to get into the entertainment industry in some behind-the-scenes capacity.

Shortly after moving to L.A., she was invited to attend a weekend seminar held at the college. This was her first glimpse of the rising star known as Mondhi. He was gaining great popularity with the college crowd, and word of his powers began to drift down through the Rodeo Drive community. He said he saw something very special in Romie, and she fell headlong under his charismatic spell. She lived and breathed for her next appointed time to study under him.

About six months after moving to Los Angeles, she received a telegram from some neighbors in her hometown. They were sad to have to deliver such difficult news to her, but her parents had been killed during a recent storm when a twister touched down on their tiny farm. In only moments, the twister killed both her mother and father and destroyed everything they had worked for. Romie was now an orphan with no other living relatives and most certainly, no good reason ever to return to her hometown again. When she allowed herself to reflect upon this moment, she noted she felt something die inside her. Then a sensation of overwhelming anticipation overtook her. The idea of a new life and a new persona started to take root. The thought made her giddy with excitement; but, where should she begin and who should she become?

Mondhi swept into her thoughts in an instant, as if he were supernaturally appointed her mentor. She clung to his every word and gesture. He became her navigator into another realm.

She looked more intently into her mirror and smiled back at her reflection.

"Romie, you really are from another realm," she said aloud to her reflection.

She tugged playfully at a long, blonde ringlet that gently cascaded down her graceful neck. She couldn't help but laugh as she reflected upon what she considered her prior existence on the farm. As a child, she had cursed fate for randomly placing her in such austere surroundings and for birthing her from such an impaired gene pool. She whiled away hours in an imaginary world of her own creation; a world that revolved around her entitlement to power, wealth, and beauty. Neither family nor friends knew anything about Romie's inner conflict.

"Five minutes, Miss Rogers." A flat voice interrupted the audio input from the studio.

She could feel the familiar surge of power rushing through her veins. She attached her monogrammed lapel pin onto her fuchsia, silk Azam suit. It fit her slim, athletic figure perfectly. Her designer collection of clothing was purposely constructed to portray elegance, sophistication, and a touch of innocence. Every detail, from her hair to her hemline, was fashioned to elicit confidence, a Southern comfortable intimacy, from the audience. There was to be absolutely no external evidence of the power-driven businesswoman beneath. The depth of her insatiable thirst for power and wealth were known only to her and, of course, her spirit guide. After all, he had helped her to ruthlessly murder the shell of a person that she had been born into and reach into her own divinity to create her higher self.

Romie Rogers had always existed in the other realm, her spirit guide had encouraged her. He merely allowed her to finally emerge and claim her rightful place in this universe.

"One minute, Miss Rogers."

Romie took one last drag from her imported Unigold Stik and extinguished it in her personal trash disposal. It wouldn't do for the queen of the airways to be discovered indulging in such a decadent habit albeit the one little vice that she allowed herself. She vowed she would quit if it ever appeared this habit might make the news in any way. But she didn't need to worry about that now. Her security guards were paid extremely well to protect her privacy, and that included personally monitoring everyone who had access to her dressing room, limo, homes, and any place where Romie might be visiting. She considered the financial extravagance to be money well spent for her own peace of mind. She had avoided any personal scandal all these years, and she intended to keep things that way.

As she got up to leave for the studio, she looked back into the mirror one last time, as was her habit.

"Hi, y'all," she purred, as she practiced her patented salute to the audience. Her perfect, Southern smile gleamed back at her. She was in control.

Something in that smile momentarily held people in its grasp. Her eyes. Something very sinister and cold flashed from behind her almost translucent emerald green eyes and then disappeared. Of course, not very many people ever got the opportunity to get that close to Romie.

# CHAPTER NINE

U NIGOLD 2000, THE smooth stik!"

One of the beautiful people smiled contentedly into the camera as she casually stepped into her flashy convertible and sped off into the sunset with an equally handsome young man at her side.

"How can they continue to advertise that trash on television?" Sara clicked off the TV and angrily tossed the remote onto the sofa cushions in the family room.

"What's it going to take for our country to decide that legalizing an instrument of death like these plant stiks is quickly reducing our youth to senseless zombies? It seems as if everything that our parents' generation fought for in getting the tobacco companies censured has gone to waste. They thought they were winning the battle against the tobacco conglomerates and helping to educate the population about the dangers of cigarette smoking. But they seem to have lost the war."

Sara had very strong feelings about this issue for more than one reason. Her father had been a fairly heavy smoker throughout his life. When the evidence of cigarette's cancer-causing elements became public knowledge, he tried to quit. He did, eventually, but it was a difficult road. He didn't realize, and the tobacco companies would not admit it, but their products were very addictive. When he finally won the battle over his addiction, he thought he was free and clear. His family was so proud of him. Shortly thereafter, he discovered he had lung cancer. It advanced quickly but before the cancer could claim another victim, he and his wife were involved in a tragic and fatal auto accident. Sara's father had been enrolled in an experimental program specifically designed for lung cancer patients. He and his wife were on their way to Arizona to start treatment when the accident occurred.

Sara never forgot the aching feeling she had felt in her heart when he had first been diagnosed. She couldn't forget the devastation that his premature death would have had on her mother. It was so senseless. *How could human beings do these things to one another, all in the name of the almighty dollar? How could the leaders of those companies sleep at night, knowing that every minute some young person was lighting up for the first time?* The conglomerates had figured out a way to legally produce the common man's drug of choice and were pocketing billions of dollars at the public's expense.

What bothered Sara so much now was how the tobacco companies had re-invented themselves and their products to fit the health-conscious climate of today. Years ago, a flurry of multi-million dollar lawsuits had dogged the industry. The tobacco industry was publicly shown to be aware of the life-threatening consequences of using their products. They were given a slap on the wrist by the legal system. They instituted more label warnings and cut back on their advertising. A momentary lull followed in the public's view of smoking and smokers.

The industry was not, however, cowering in a corner licking its wounds. Insider information later disclosed that the six major producers of smoking materials around the globe had secretly formed a research coalition. They had been redirecting a percentage of their profits for some years into the research and development of a new type of tobacco plant. They had assembled a team of leading scientists in the field of plant genetics to produce a totally new breed of smoking material.

In the process of their experimentation, they had been successful in altering the tobacco leaves so they produced no harmful carcinogens when smoked. They introduced the genetics of other plants into their makeup to enhance flavor, smoothness, and reduce smoke inhaled into the lungs and expelled into the atmosphere. The new plants were almost unrecognizable when compared to traditional tobacco plants. By developing this new breed of super plant, they had also found a way to cut down their overhead. These plants were hardy and prolific.

They had managed to produce an entirely new smokable plant. They passed the most stringent governmental agency testing for cancer-causing agents. Their products were now so environmentally friendly that their advertising campaign could take a whole new approach. Since the plants were engineered to adopt the properties of other herbs, spices, and florals, the new products were touted as being a new vehicle for personal aromatherapy.

The tobacco industry had succeeded in totally re-inventing cigarettes. Now they were called nature stiks, or "stiks" for short. All the proponents of making the environment a more pleasant space were graciously courted by the consortium of manufacturers. These new smoke stiks were scientifically proven to be absolutely no relation to the cigarettes of two decades ago. The Chamomile Stiks for instance, were healthy, natural, and even described as producing an aura of calm and serenity about the user. Even Senator Nash Brookline was seen smoking a Unigold 2000 on Capitol Hill when they were first introduced to the American public. He said that he looked forward to the aromatherapy working wonders on the floor of Congress to soothe the "savage beast."

Sara couldn't help but wonder what agenda was lurking beneath this sudden beneficent attitude adopted by the former tobacco manufacturers. She hadn't had time to explore the newly developed plants herself, but she had an ominous feeling about what she might discover if she were to probe more deeply into the potential side effects of these new stiks.

# CHAPTER TEN

THE HUGE ENGINES of the Concourse 201 powered up. Romie sipped Dom Perignon from a crystal champagne flute and gazed out the window. First Class had its perks and she had worked a lifetime to achieve this preferred status. She chuckled to herself. She had actually taken one lifetime, used it, and then discarded it to produce this new life for herself. Her spirit guide had been right at every turn. He convinced her that the benefits accorded her new identity were what her karma had destined for her from time immemorial. Life was full of sensual experiences to be devoured, power to be harnessed, and immortality to be attained at any cost.

She took another sip of champagne and followed it with a bite from the luscious red strawberry that floated in her glass. Her pulse quickened as she imagined the outcome of this little excursion.

This flight to Sydney, Australia, was being publicly reported as part business and part pleasure. She was scheduled to meet with several television executives there to arrange her upcoming remote taping in Sydney and to meet some of the potential guests for her one-week show taping next fall. That had satisfied the media and her associates. The remaining few days were to be spent luxuriating at Spa Divino, a highly exclusive enclave, which catered to the rich and famous from around the globe. Celebrities from every arena made pilgrimages to the Spa's famed kelp baths and returned home looking years younger and totally refreshed. Of course, the owners of Spa Divino were extremely discrete and never, ever divulged the names of guests. Rumors had arisen about the Divinos as well, since they judiciously avoided any kind of publicity. They were rarely seen in public, and some believed the couple preferred the rarified air of their spa environment and it kept them looking young. They never seemed to age at all.

Romie had personally made her reservations with Serge Divino. She did not want anyone to know the true purpose behind her visit to the Spa. Over the years, she had made many powerful connections with the movers and shakers around the globe. Her celebrity, her power in the media, and, of course, her financial wizardry had afforded her contact with some of the most notorious power brokers in the world. Her spirit guide had always advised her about whom to contact and when. He would advise her when someone was about to fall out of favor or was about to experience financial ruin and would arrange for her to discretely intervene. She would seem to them to be a beneficent angel, dropped fortuitously into their lives at their lowest point. She would always have a solution for their situation and they, of course, would be eternally grateful.

Her guide had instructed her well in the art of favors for favors. Oftentimes she had no idea how a certain relationship would ultimately benefit her, but she remained confident that her guide knew what the future would bring. She had not been disappointed yet.

It was one of these favors that brought her to Sydney and especially to Spa Divino. The Spa was a luxury that she looked forward to with great anticipation. Her grueling schedule this year had indeed left her exhausted. The prospect of being pampered for three days was heavenly. But before she would allow herself to indulge in this reward, she had one pressing appointment she had to keep. Serge Divino was the brother of Doctor Balfor Divino, a renowned research scientist who had perfected the art of genetic cloning with humans.

Dr. Divino had established a laboratory deep in the Australian Outback. He had designed a place where he could continue to develop and refine his theories and research without concern for public outcry or invasion from the prying eyes of the paparazzi. He had developed a method of cloning that allowed for any man or woman to procreate without the need of human contact from the opposite sex. He could extract sufficient DNA from any individual and guarantee them a baby that would be their total and complete clone. Identical in every way possible.

He had also gone one step further. He had produced an artificial womb environment. The fetus, created in a test tube, could be transferred into the "womb" and left there until the gestation period was over. He had so refined this procedure that anyone who opted for this method could take their artificial womb home with them and, with simple instructions, maintain the environment, nutrients, and monitoring systems. A specially designed computer monitored everything, and when "delivery" was imminent, they would be alerted that it was time to remove the fully developed baby from its container. The parent or parents could have some choice in their child's "birthday" because all this was carefully pre-determined during the interview time at the laboratory.

Wealthy men and women from around the globe sought out Dr. Divino to take advantage of what his science had provided for civilization. Still, a great deal of controversy surrounded his work. The scientific community had initially been extremely hesitant to believe he had finally achieved the impossible. But he proved that his experiments worked when he produced his first "Aqua Baby" as he called her. Serge and his wife Nita had wanted to have children but were unable to conceive. Nita was Dr. Divino's first clone parent. The baby, Nina, was perfect. The top medical research doctors worldwide examined her. The experiment was no longer a theory. It was a reality.

The scientific community rallied behind Dr. Divino. He was awarded the prestigious Crystal Flame Award, the highest honor awarded by the Global Community for work that would impact the future of humankind and ultimately allow man to achieve his full potential.

Despite all the publicity, Dr. Divino preferred to maintain his privacy and that of his patients at all costs. Although many of his patients were initially infertile couples who wanted children, the complexion of his client base quickly changed dramatically. Soon individuals who were not interested in the state of matrimony were seeking out his clinic. Heads of state, movie stars, athletes, and anyone with the financial ability to underwrite the procedure were making treks to his remote facility. Dr. Divino always maintained that his interest was purely in the medical capability of providing a solution to a human need. He never allowed himself to delve into the motives of his patients. He saw himself merely as a humble servant of mankind. He had discovered how to meet a primal need of humanity without outside influences. He was neither a philosopher nor a religious person. He left the morals of mankind to the individual.

But there were some who tried to influence public opinion by debating the morality and the scientific necessity of such procedures. The airwaves were continually abuzz with heated, passionate discussions about the long-term effects of Dr. Divino's achievements. Medical ethicists and scientists around the globe continued to debate the ever-ascending list of concerns as it appeared that mankind desired to open more of these expensive clinics around the world. They expressed concerns about the genetic codes of one-parent offspring and their ultimate effects upon evolution. They cited as examples the myriad problems that had arisen over the centuries as men continued to closely breed dogs and other animals. The original and desirable characteristics had often disappeared, and physical and mental aberrations had taken their place.

Dr. Divino's detractors were concerned about the ultimate toll upon the parents of the cloned children. They had many questions: How does the parent relate to a child who is essentially "you," but without any life experiences? Does the parent only and forever see their own character flaws reflected in the child? Does the parent end up treating the child too harshly as they attempt to drive out their own personal demons? Does a woman suddenly wake up one morning, a forty-year-old single mother (by choice) and see a twenty-year-old vibrant, exact version of herself with all the natural imperfections erased? Does the woman become enraged with jealousy at now having to compete with her "perfect" self? And even more bizarre, what would happen if both husband and wife decided to clone themselves to produce two offspring? What if the two children, a boy and a girl, are attracted to one another when they grow older? What would happen to the very fabric of the family.... the very fabric of humanity?

The self-actualization gurus gloriously espoused each new development. They preached that this was the ultimate expression of the god within each person. They believed this science proved they were right all along. Man is indeed a god and now has proven his own divinity by finally discovering and claiming the ability to create life independent of all traditional methods.

They never asked themselves what becomes of the soul? Does each cloned child have its own spirit and soul divinely implanted at conception? How will society now define "birth"? Is it merely a time of convenience exacted by the scientists determining that the cloned fetus is deemed to be "ripe" for harvesting from its moist, artificial, chemical environment of nourishment? Since it must grow in this artificial environment, instead of hearing its mother's soothing heartbeat, it will hear synthesized recreations of a maternal heartbeat. Instead of being soothed by the continual movement of its mother, its womb environment will be gently vibrated by some computer generated movement. Is there any room in this new world for primal maternal bonding at birth? Does this child possess any physical, emotional, or spiritual identification with its mother when it is "born"? And what will the eternal and future consequences be for society?

The Divino brothers, satisfied they had fixed their place in history and, as was their family motto, turned their eyes to the horizon and never looked back.

# CHAPTER ELEVEN

TINY RIVULETS OF rain etched glorious prisms of moving color down the length of the observation windows at Noah and Sara's favorite beachside restaurant, The Ledge. Its unique architectural design had been the focus of many magazine articles and news pieces throughout the years. The owner, James Camroth, had inherited it from his father years ago. He had maintained the family traditions of excellence and innovation with new advances each year. Noah and Sara enjoyed the ambience the most. The Ledge seemed to hover in mid-air over the Southern California coastline. The unusual design of The Ledge reminded one of a giant bronze and glass saucer protruding from the cliff overlooking the ocean, supported by a complex web of steel spines beneath it, which anchored it securely into bedrock. The bronze color of the metal outer structure was chosen for how it reflected the setting sun's rays, bathing the entire structure in an ethereal glow each evening. It maintained an attitude of luxury and tranquility often overlooked in the present day hustle and bustle of the typical coastal communities. James had recently made an extensive addition to the outdoor balcony dining area. The balcony extended out along the entire outer rim of the restaurant. He designed and installed a retractable wall and ceiling of glass, which could be moved or removed by the press of a button. It provided his clientele with the ability to dine waterside in any weather condition with an unobstructed view, allowing the soothing sounds of the surf and the wind to mesmerize them during their leisurely dining experience. Since the entire restaurant was in the shape of a giant arc, which seemed to literally be growing out of the adjoining cliff, this new addition made for some of the most spectacular sunsets anywhere on the West Coast.

As Noah reached across the linen tablecloth to pour Sara a glass of their favorite Merlot, she motioned for him to put the bottle down and took his hand in hers.

"Noah, I can't believe how lucky we are and how much we have to be thankful for in our lives."

"I agree, Sara. We have three sons who are passionate men with purpose in their lives, and three of the most wonderful daughters-in-law that anyone could hope for." He gave her hands a slight squeeze. "I guess that's part of the allure of this place for us. Each time we come here and take in the majesty of the ocean and the skyline, listen to the waves and feel the ocean breezes drift in, it's impossible to avoid lingering on all the things for which we are grateful. And I, for one, am most grateful for my best friend, my partner, and my beautiful wife."

Still holding hands across the table, they were both distracted by the silent retraction of the glass walls and ceiling that had been protecting them from the light rain that had just fallen. Both instinctively drew in deep breaths of the fresh night air, which mingled the saltiness of the ocean with the refreshing aroma of rainfall, a heady combination. Noah and Sara continued to talk about the boys and their individual projects. They were both so pleased that Shem would be able to stay with them for a while during his upcoming sabbatical. His wife would soon be joining them, and they were all looking forward to spending some family time out on their boat fishing.

"Noah, I forgot to tell you that Jake called, and he and Gloria will be flying in to town in a few days. He said he had some amazing news to share. He mentioned that his work had led him into the Rift Valley."

"I remember him talking about that area a few years ago," Noah said. "What did he call it? The hidden Garden of Eden, I think. Anyway, he was concerned because there were two large tribes that had been warring over a certain area for decades. One wanted to level the land, destroy the lush and unique vegetation, and make a treaty with a neighboring country's oil and land developers. They said they wanted to bring their newly formed country into this century. But the other tribe was fighting to retain their habitat and find alternative means to bolster their economy while retaining their bargaining position in the world markets."

"If I recall, there was one area in particular that interested Jake more than any other. There was a stand of trees of enormous proportions unlike anything else in the area. It was located in the central area of dispute between the tribes and had become a symbol for each tribe in their quest for supremacy." Sara drew in a deep breath and sighed. "I believe that Jake said that the trees were referred to by their ancient name, gopher wood trees. The locals believe that their gods had planted this stand eons ago and that these trees had been genetically designed to withstand all forms of disease and weather."

"I'm sure Jake will have plenty of stories to tell when he gets home," smiled Noah. His gaze again locked with Sara's.

Thunder shook them as lightning squirreled across the sky. Both swiveled to look back at the ocean. A full moon hung directly above the water. The panoramic view was so clear that it felt like you might see all the way to the curvature of the earth. There had been no ominous cloud formations earlier in the evening, just a light sprinkle of rain.

"Noah, did you feel that rumble beneath us?"

"I thought it was just that feeling you get when you're startled by thunder."

"There it is again." Sara grabbed Noah's arm and held tightly.

This time something very bad was happening. He looked past Sara and could barely glimpse the side of the cliff beyond her, where the restaurant jutted out from the rocks and dirt. He closed his eyes and reopened them as if to clear his head. Was he seeing what he thought or was his imagination playing tricks on him? Rivers of water rushed from beneath the surface of the rocks and hard-packed dirt of the cliff on which the restaurant sat. And the water intensity was increasing.

Sara grabbed his arm tighter. This time the entire restaurant shook. *Could this be the "big one"? Was this the big earthquake that many doomsayers predicted so frequently would destroy all of California?* Whatever it was, they needed to make a hasty exit to safety. As Noah lifted Sara from the banquette, he saw the terror in her brown eyes. He turned to see what had captured her attention. He looked over his shoulder to see something on the horizon. He then looked down beneath the edge of the restaurant and saw the waves were withdrawing from the shore. They were not coming back in. He looked back again towards the horizon and he immediately knew he had seen this image before.

On the edge of his field of vision a very large, very black wall formed, spreading across the horizon and simultaneously reaching skyward at blistering speed.

Lightning crackled across the sky, first in one direction, then the opposite, and finally straight down, illuminating the watery monster rushing toward the shore.

The next sound to assault Noah's ears was the restaurant bowing and twisting. He could see the sides of the cliffs being destroyed by the rush of water emerging from the very depths of the earth. They were trapped between this unforgiving monster from the deep blindly running to inundate the coast, while the coast itself was yielding to some internal liquefaction causing it to crumble back into the ocean. The increasing noise of the rushing tsunami and the crashing of the cliffs around them was far greater than a hundred jet engines.

Noah heard screaming. Was it his voice? Was it Sara? His chest felt like a giant weight had settled on it. His lungs were raw from his own screams for help.

# Chapter Twelve

"NOAH, NOAH, NOAH."

He bolted upright. He was drenched in sweat. The hair on the back of his neck stood straight up. He awoke so abruptly that he almost fell off of the sofa in his office. He tried to stand and get his bearings. Noah barely remembered going into his office to get some papers after dinner. He must have fallen asleep. *Was this a dream? A vision? Was he awake or still asleep? How could anything feel so real and so terrifying at the same time?*

"Noah."

Someone called his name. But who? A profound fear mixed with awe filled the room. His vision must be playing tricks on him because it seemed his surroundings dissolved into a mist. This brilliant mist was growing and building before his eyes. The brightness became intolerable. He raised his hands to shield his eyes, but to no avail. The brilliance penetrated his entire being. The sound emanating from the brilliance was all encompassing. This sound wasn't coming to his brain as sound would normally travel through the ears and into his senses. This sound penetrated his very cells.

As the experience continued, Noah found it impossible to remain on his feet. He found himself face down on the floor of his office. His body trembled uncontrollably. Yet, mixed with this awesome presence, brilliant light, and unearthly sound, there descended upon him a peace that he had never experienced in his entire life. Expectancy now filled the room.

"Noah."

He had heard the unmistakable voice before in his dreams. This time, there was the same authority, but an authority enveloped in a compassion that felt comforting beyond any previous experience. It caused his spirit to settle down enough to answer.

"Here I am," Noah tentatively offered into the air without daring to lift his face off the tile floor.

"Noah, my son."

The words hovered in mid-air. They had a resonance that made Noah feel like someone had hit a tuning fork and his body and mind began to resonate in confirmation with this voice. It felt like nothing he'd ever experienced before, and yet as natural as breathing. Although, at this moment his breathing was more in the form of gasps and gulps.

"Noah, I have treasured the times of intimacy that I have spent with you in this very place over the years. My Spirit has never been far from you. You are a man after my own heart."

*This cannot be.* Every part of Noah's being and spirit cried out for more. But his analytical mind screamed back that this could not be happening. This could not be happening to him; not here; not now. *This could not be the voice of ... he could scarcely think the word ... God.*

"Fear not, my son. You know my voice. You have touched my heart as I have touched yours since before you were born. I have found you righteous and blameless. I have set you apart, you and your family. I am about to destroy all creation because it has become detestable and filled with violence. I will replenish the earth once again. And I will allow my love and mercy and compassion to flow freely. That is why I have chosen you and your family to prepare for the coming disaster."

Suddenly, as if clouds in his mind cleared away, Noah knew what the dreams had been. It became evident in that instant that all that he and Sara had observed over the years was not their imagination, it was real. The earth had become an enemy of God. And God was about to set things right. But the cost was beyond his ability to comprehend at this moment.

"Don't let your heart be troubled with confusion. I will make all these things clear as I lay out the course that you will travel. The time is short, but I will reveal each step that you are to take to accomplish the task ahead. I will destroy the earth with a flood. You and your family alone will survive. In order to succeed, you will build a ship unlike anything man has seen before. To the world, you and this ship will appear to be the ultimate in foolishness. This ship will be 450 feet long, by 75 feet wide by 45 feet high. It will consist of lower, middle, and upper decks, with a roof and a door on the side. It will be constructed of gopher wood, and you will seal it as I instruct you, with pitch. When it is finished, I will bring two of every kind to enter this ship. There will be room for provisions, water, and ventilation. I will reveal more details as time approaches. Now, rest. I will write all these instructions upon your heart, and they will become clearer with each day."

As suddenly as His presence had filled the room, it was gone. Noah could feel the comforting, cool smoothness of the tiled office floor pressing against his flushed face. He took a deep breath. He was drained and all he wanted to do was to lie there and await consciousness. This too had been just a dream.

# CHAPTER THIRTEEN

NOAH STRETCHED HIS muscular frame to its full length and stretched his arms high above his head. As he did, a warm burgundy chenille throw slid to the floor.

"Oh." Noah dragged out the lone syllable of that simple word as he pressed his fingers against his cheek before massaging the back of his neck. "This getting to be over fifty has a down side, I guess. Mornings are getting a little more difficult" he murmured to himself, almost fully awake.

The neon green numbers on his digital table clock showed 6 a.m. One thing that had always been consistent about Noah was his internal body clock. Even in college, with all the late-night study sessions, he could always wake up at this time. It drove Sara to distraction because not only could he do this consistently, without the need of an alarm clock, but when he awakened, he was fully functional *and* cheerful. Today was no exception. The glorious Southern California sun cascaded through the windows of the work area that he shared with Sara. He could hear morning doves outside and could even catch the slightest hint of ocean breeze wafting through one of the open windows at the end of the room.

He padded barefoot over to the bathroom area, which separated his work area from Sara's. Without glancing in the mirror, he ran some cold, crisp water into the sink. They were very lucky because the local drinking water was supplied from dozens of nearby deep springs, so the tap water was not only icy cold when it came out but tasted better than any bottled water. He began splashing his face and then ran his wet fingers through his full, wavy hair. So much for taming the bedhead monster. He reached behind him and fumbled the thirsty towel off the hook on the wall. Vigorously rubbing his face, he finally glanced at his reflection in the mirror. He stopped abruptly. The reflection staring back at him was familiar yet held something more. He traced his fingers gingerly across his cheeks.

"Ouch!" His left cheek was a bit sore. He couldn't remember why at this moment. He traced around the corners of his eyes. There was something different in his eyes. He felt a little self-conscious at this extraordinary self-examination, but he couldn't stop himself.

He stepped back two paces to get a better perspective on what he was seeing. There was something more. It seemed like he looked refreshed, rested, a little flushed maybe. While his body was experiencing some soreness from sleeping on the sofa, it simultaneously felt invigorated. He stared into the mirror more closely. If he didn't know better, he'd say that he had a certain glow about him. Very subtle, but very vigorous. And there was a determination and depth in his eyes that he had never noticed before.

"Enough of this," he whispered to himself. If Sara or the boys ever caught him spending this much time in front of a mirror they'd wonder what had happened to him and what he'd done with the real Noah Arcmann. He remembered that Shem was here and his wife Hope had probably arrived very late last night. Jake and Gloria probably arrived very early this morning. "I guess maybe they do have some of my better character traits," he said aloud with a smile.

He gradually noticed he was famished and there must be a

large cup of some bold, Brazilian blend coffee calling his name. He always looked forward to times when the entire family was gathered together. Mealtimes were notoriously rowdy and filled with conversations covering the globe, good-natured ribbing, and plenty of laughter. Yes, mealtimes were always his favorite time to spend with his family. Noah considered it to be such a rare blessing that Gloria, Hope, and Joy, Ham's wife, fit in so smoothly. They could hold their own in any contest of wit and add interesting and insightful commentary with the family on a variety of topics. Like their husbands and Noah and Sara, the girls' interests crossed a broad spectrum of topics. The boys used to tease that if the four Arcmann men could ever be a team on one of those famous trivia information television shows, they could probably make a clean sweep.

"Shy, quiet, and retiring wouldn't be the best adjectives to describe the Arcmann boys," he mused to himself, stifling a chuckle.

Sweet, pungent notes of strong coffee, and eggs and sizzling bacon greeted his senses as he approached the expansive kitchen and family room area. Sara was busying herself over the stove and checking on the biscuits that Gloria had placed in the oven. Gloria and Jake were ensconced on one of the overstuffed sofas with coffee mugs steaming in hand. Shem was stretched out in one of the two leather chairs facing the wall of windows overlooking the back of the property.

The round, custom-made koa wood table that the family used for informal dining was set. A flight of nostalgia swept over Noah as he remembered his father-son project with Jake one summer. Their old dining table had withstood the tumult of years serving three boys growing up and it was beginning to show its age. Jake was already quite the carpenter and wanted to do something very special for Christmas for his mom. So he convinced Noah they could design a perfectly round table with enough additional leaves to make it possible to accommodate at least twelve when it was extended to full length. This seemed to be quite a daunting proposal, but Noah knew better than to try to discourage Jake from a project once he had set his mind on it. Before he knew it, Jake had done some investigating and some amazing networking provided them with just enough koa wood from Hawaii to build this masterpiece. They worked on it every spare moment in their well-equipped workshop located in a large converted shed at the far side of the property. It provided them the opportunity to work without Sara being able to see the surprise and they could work early or late, at will. There was little that Jake and Noah loved more than the smell of freshly cut lumber and the feel of raw wood being planed by hand into a new and beautifully utilitarian design. By Christmas Eve that year, an exquisite piece of furniture sat boldly in the middle of the workshop. Hours of painstaking hand sanding, oiling, and buffing had produced a work of art. The finish was so amazing that a person could see their reflection in it. The largest scarlet red bow sat atop it, waiting for Christmas morning when they would escort an unsuspecting Sara to the workshop. Noah wasn't sure who was more excited that Christmas, Jake or him.

Noah shook his head as if shaking himself back to the present would help take in all that was going on in the family room. This is what he had so looked forward to. But something was not right. The atmosphere was eerily quiet. Not one person was talking. Noah looked more closely at each family member, and it seemed that each was deeply lost in their own thoughts. And, unlike their usual habit, no one was sharing.

# CHAPTER FOURTEEN

NOAH'S CELL PHONE nearly vibrated off the edge of the dining table. He always kept the ringer set to the old-fashioned ring of the early dial type phones so he would be sure to hear it, even if he didn't feel the initial vibration of an incoming call. At this particular moment, the shrill ring and the sight of the vibrating phone about to jump off the edge of the table caught everyone by surprise and shook them all back to the present.

Noah flipped open the phone with one smooth movement before he even had time to notice the caller I.D.

"Dad, it's Ham and Joy," both voices chimed in over the phone. "We just wanted to give you a head's up. We've come down the canyon and will be at the house in ten minutes. Hold breakfast for us, will you? We're starving."

Noah didn't even get a chance to respond when Ham clicked off, or maybe he just dropped the call in the canyon area. Ham and Joy had been called in by Sara to join the team working with Biosphere Five. Sara and Noah wanted to make as extensive an evaluation as possible as to the progress being made at the Biosphere so far. As fate would have it, the Department of Global Ecological Management had skirted all local laws and had more than a thousand acres of private land declared National Forest so they could establish the Biosphere Dome. Noah and Sara's acreage abutted this newly established National Forest.

Years ago Sara had set aside at least twenty acres at the eastern-most edge of their property where it gently folded into the forest for her own agricultural experimentation with crop rotation and land resuscitation. While their home and land were not readily visible from the coastal highway, because they were located just behind an outcropping of trees, the Arcmann home was only a few miles from Biosphere Five, as the crow flies.

For several years, Global Resource Management had been importing various dwindling and exotic plant life and animal species to the Biosphere. Their experiments were meant to find a way to genetically enhance both so they could return to the ever-changing world climate with the effects of encroaching civilization and be able to survive and thrive. The scientists had gone so far as to try to engineer the various DNA strands of some of the animals so they could coexist with other species once thought to be their mortal enemies and therefore be relocated to parts of the globe to prosper where they would otherwise have perished. From Sara's perspective, this was all very much like bad science fiction. But as Ham and Noah observed, the global environment was changing at such a rapid pace that the government and scientific community was not beyond taking the wildest theories and trying to make them work.

In his pursuit of the position of Global First Citizen, President Hy Wells and his premier supporter, Senator Nash Brookline, had been spearheading the promotional work for Biosphere Five. That's why they had invited the Arcmann family of scientists to become involved. Wells and Brookline needed more structure and down-to-earth science to keep this project alive even after sinking billions of dollars into it. And they desperately wanted to have the Arcmann family name representing traditional scientific values and approach associated with their investment. Regardless of how the Arcmanns' personal values were at absolute odds with almost everything that Wells and Brookline stood for, they thought they could at least find some common ground in the Arcmanns' productive work to save plants, land, and animal life across the continents. The family was well respected in their various fields of expertise and GEM could put up with a lot in order to resurrect this project and bring it back into vogue.

Noah flipped his cell phone closed and stuffed it into the pocket of his jeans. Looking up, he noticed that everyone in the room had been wrested from their previous contemplations and now curiously stared at him. This only lasted a moment and then everyone began talking almost at one time.

"Come on, family. Come and get it while it's hot." Sara offered.

Noah was thankful for a return to some normalcy for the moment. And he truly was famished as he had noticed much earlier. He walked over to get a cup from the cupboard just in front of Sara. Reaching past her, he managed to kiss her gently on her forehead.

"Good morning, sweetheart. Aren't you glad I found you asleep in the office last night and threw that cover over you so you wouldn't freeze?" Sara playfully swiped at him with the serving spoon in her hand and giggled. Her gaze into his eyes lingered longer than normal.

"What's wrong, sweetie? Do I still have a terminal case of bedhead? I thought I cleaned up fairly well this morning before coming in here," Noah retorted with a crinkle of his deep blue eyes.

"Nothing." She kept staring. "Nothing at all, really. You just seem a little different somehow. I must be seeing things or maybe I'm just too excited about having all the family together under one roof for a while. Don't mind me. Let's get this breakfast going."

Sara picked up a large ceramic serving bowl filled to the brim with her special scrambled eggs with diced green onion and finely sliced smoked salmon. The delicious mingling aromas of salmon, eggs, and onions had long been an Arcmann family favorite for special breakfasts, and today each of them seemed to need something familiar to embrace.

Jake and Gloria extricated themselves from the sofa and came over to Noah to give him a big bear hug hello.

"What have you been up to, Dad? You look like you've been on a retreat or a vacation or something," Jake said as Gloria nodded in assent. "Whatever it is, it agrees with you. Hey, don't block the way to Gloria's homemade biscuits!" Jake and Gloria each picked up a basket of the freshly baked treats and went to find a place at the table.

Shem meanwhile had unfolded himself from his perch in the leather chair and was graciously escorting his wife Hope to their places at the table. Noah picked up the coffee pot, offered refills to everyone, and went back to prepare another pot so there would be enough for Ham and Joy when they arrived. He no sooner started opening the coffee canister to make another pot when the front door burst open and Ham and Joy came rushing in to join the family gathering. Everyone got up and for a brief moment, got lost in the entanglement of arms, kisses "hello," and ruffled hair that Noah liked to call "Norman Rockwell" moments. The snapshot of love can't easily be put into words. But for now, all felt very right with the world.

# CHAPTER FIFTEEN

A MIDST THE SEA of microphone booms and clicking cameras, Romie Rogers burst through the airport doorway and headed for her personal limousine while flashing that world-renowned smile. One microphone managed to emerge from the rest, and attached to it was Rionne Sanders from the six o'clock news.

"Miss Rogers! Miss Rogers! You look absolutely radiant. Rumor has it that you retreated to Sydney for some new and unexplored beauty treatments. Can you comment for our audience?" Rionne pressed as close to Romie as bodyguards would allow.

"Why darlin', you know me better than that." Romie smiled directly into the cameras. "I was just preparing for my next series of the *Romie Rogers Show* to be shot in Sydney in the fall. I do believe that good, hard work is the only beauty treatment that I could ever need."

On cue, her bodyguards whisked her into the limousine and she was engulfed in her shiny, black invulnerable chariot and gone. The media was her toy and she manipulated it as exquisitely as a symphony conductor leads his orchestra.

Romie turned to her chief security guard, Otto. "You have your instructions. Make certain that you personally track my little jewel's trip to my estate. I don't want any slip ups and absolutely no cameras. When it arrives, I want it taken directly to the nursery and all the connections to the Internet established and double-checked. Make certain the redundancy battery backup and nutrition stations are working appropriately. Did you run a complete system check before we left for Sydney, like I asked?" Romie's sweet Southern drawl evaporated at times like these in the privacy of her own little world. But she was cognizant of this minor flaw and was working desperately to maintain her drawl permanently. She almost had it. The excitement of bringing her "baby" home was just too much for the moment. She had to regain her aloofness. "It will be just wonderful, honey," she drawled to herself under her breath as she absentmindedly switched on the Internet monitor in her limousine.

Away from the prying eyes and cameras of the paparazzi, an exquisitely designed set of luggage was being loaded into a special windowless black van at the airport. From a distance, it resembled any of a number of designer luggage ensembles the jet set favored; until you pressed close, and then you saw something very unusual. At the lower left-hand corner of each bag was a small, rose-colored, inverted triangular shaped mirror. Wrapped along the outside edge was a beautifully etched black velvet rose with iridescent leaves and glistening gold thorns protruding from the stem. Romie had her own designer hand make each piece to her exact specifications, including this very newest piece. It appeared to be large enough to cradle a substantial home aquarium and had hard sides and stabilizers built into the frame. It was temperature controlled to within a tenth of a degree. On the outside it resembled the old wardrobes on casters found on ocean liners. Nothing out of the normal. Nothing, that is, for Romie.

Romie had left off the volume to her monitor so she didn't notice that as soon as her interview with Rionne was finished, the network switched to a feed from the Micro Global Access Connection. GAC was running a live feed from another "Dead Man Curls" event off Hawaii. Clips of the Riders enveloped inside a monstrous tsunami, riding at break neck speed into the shore were at once vile and, yet, like the scene of an accident, drew you in so that you couldn't avert your eyes. A local reporter cut to his interview with Skiff Borden, the leader of the Riders.

"Skiff, what do you think about the dozens of new Riders that came out today to join you? At last count, we have at least four that we know never made it into shore."

"What a rush. They are the real heroes." Borden gasped as water dripped from his toned body. "They knew how to live on the edge. They played the wave and the wave won. But they died players. They had the guts to feel what it's like to take your life into your own hands; to feel your blood rushing through your veins and to look destiny in the face. I can't wait for the next Dead Man Curls event."

Skiff glared directly into the camera as if challenging the world to go into battle with this ungodly force of nature and despising anyone too terrified to join him and his team. His eyes flashed black, coal black and deathly blank, into the camera lens, and just as suddenly back to his natural deep green.

"We heard that you and the Riders will be going over to the other side of the island later today to ride the volcano. Is there anything you can tell us about this new thrill?" The reporter pressed in closer to Skiff.

Skiff broadened his smile. "It's just another way of tempting the gods. The water will be about 400 degrees. One wrong move and—" He snapped his fingers. "Poof, boiled. The trick is to paddle through it, ride it for as long as you can, before your board starts to melt. I'll see you on the other side."

He pumped his fist in the air to arouse the gathered crowd. As he waved goodbye, you could just barely make out the inverted triangle with the letters, "TE" emblazoned on his palm. And then the connection dropped.

# CHAPTER SIXTEEN

H EY, DON'T HOG all of my wife's biscuits," Jake called across the table to Ham, who faked a go-long-for-it football pass with one.

"Haven't you girls taught my boys any manners yet?" smiled Sara across the table. "There's plenty for everyone this morning. And if any of you boys want more, I know you all know how to cook."

Relaxed laughter rippled around the room and the normal verbal gymnastics of the Arcmann clan filled the morning. Once everyone had had their fill and the cleanup had begun, the conversations began to take on a more serious note.

Ham started, "You all looked kind of strange when we arrived this morning. It didn't feel like our normal family climate when Joy and I first walked in. Anything going on that we should know about?"

Jake helped his wife rinse off the dishes and place them in the dishwasher so Sara and Noah could relax together on the sofa. Finished loading the dishwasher, Jake strolled across the great room to where the rest of the family was gathered.

"I don't know about anyone else, but I had the weirdest dream last night and I just couldn't shake it. You know how sometimes you dream something and while you're in the dream, you could swear that it was real? Well, that was what this dream, or should I say nightmare, felt like."

Noah was wrenched into the present conversation. "Tell us about it, if it's not too personal, Jake."

"Yeah, we all want a chance to delve deeply into your psyche, Jake," chided Ham.

"Okay, Dr. Freud, see what you can make of this." Jake plopped onto the floor and leaned against a stack of over stuffed tapestry pillows stacked on the floor next to one of the sofas for support. "I dreamed that you and Shem and Dad and I were on our fishing boat. But we were all very young. We hadn't been catching many fish. Then suddenly Dad got really concerned and we saw this wild black wall of water starting to rush towards the boat. We were all scared and it was almost on top of us." Jake's voice trailed off.

"Then what?" Everyone chimed in simultaneously.

"Oh, I'm sorry. The dream just ended abruptly right there. But I had this nagging sense that there was supposed to be more to it." Jake shook his head.

Noah tried desperately to hide his looming dread. This couldn't be happening.

"Well, having a scientific mind, I wouldn't generally adhere to a coincidence theory. But I am a little shocked to hear you describe exactly the same dream I had last night as well," added Shem.

"Me too!" exclaimed Ham with a look of surprise.

Noah glanced over at Sara. A brooding cloud passed across her lovely countenance.

"Sara. You look a little troubled. You couldn't possibly have had the same dream too, could you?" Noah offered tentatively.

"Before I answer, did any of you girls have that dream too?" Sara looked around the room as each of the wives nodded that they had similar dreams about their husbands. The puzzled looks on their faces made the atmosphere even more curious.

"I don't exactly know where to start. There was so much going on in this dream. Noah, you and I were dining at The Ledge on a glorious evening with a clear full moon. Suddenly, without warning, everything started coming apart. The restaurant was ripping apart, the cliffs were dissolving into the ocean and..." she paused to catch her breath. "There was a monstrous inky black tsunami crushing towards us."

Again, as if everyone was holding their collective breath, they exploded in unison, "What happened next?"

"I'm sorry. I don't remember any more. But like you said, Jake, I just couldn't shake the feelings associated with it this morning before breakfast."

Noah didn't want to explore what all this meant, and he certainly didn't want to share his dream or vision or whatever it was that he had experienced last night with anyone just yet. He needed to temporarily turn everyone's attention from this supernatural mystery and toward something tangible. He needed time to think, rationally. He needed time to meditate. Mostly, he needed some space and time to pray. Answers would most certainly follow.

"Well, that's a lot to take in so early in the morning, guys. We've all got work ahead of us, so what say we table this discussion for a little later." Noah leaned forward. "Ham, why don't you and Joy take your mom with you out to visit the Biosphere this afternoon? Get a lay of the land and come back with your suggestions of how you think we should proceed."

"I'd like to join them. Maybe Gloria and I can take our car out there as well and bring along our photo equipment to document what's been happening so far. Shem and Hope, if you wouldn't mind coming with us, we could use some help setting up all the equipment we've brought." Jake really wanted to sink his teeth into this project and see if there was any hope that the Biosphere experiment would bring a brighter future to many of the tribal lands across the globe that were suffering so much.

Noah stood up like the conductor of a small orchestra and motioned everyone to go gather their equipment and get on with their day.

"What are you going to be working on, darling?" Sara inquired as she headed to her office to pick up some gear.

"I have those plans that Global Resource Management expressed over to me. I've been studying them and I need to make some sense out of what they're trying to accomplish and how we could possibly prepare for an appropriate expansion if this proves scientifically worthy." Noah tried to keep his private concerns out of his voice.

"Don't work too hard. We'll all be back by dinner time." Sara kissed Noah lightly on the cheek and gave him a hug as she left to load the car.

Noah decided that a quick shower was a good idea. Maybe that would clear his head and give him a fresh look at the world. Within an hour he was bent over his worktable, scouring the pages of floor plans sent from GRM. The company had spent an awful lot of the taxpayers' money on this dream, but it was beginning to look like a bit of a nightmare from Noah's perspective. There just wasn't near enough room to provide adequate habitat for all these different types of animals and plants, let alone transfer them into alternate habitat to check out their theories of the potential co-existence of predators and prey. They had severely underestimated the air exchangers necessary to provide a pollutant free initial environment to welcome the specimens as they transferred in to the Biosphere.

This project appeared to have been rushed from conception to build out far too prematurely. And, as is often the case when private investors are involved with government based projects, results are all that matter. Unfortunately, the results don't need to always be positive. They just need to make for good footage on the evening news. This was looking a lot like one of those unfortunate instances.

Brain overload was beginning to set in on Noah. He got up, stretched, and paced around the office. Sara had insisted they build a mini kitchen in their work area, just big enough to hold a small refrigerator for cold drinks and a few protein snacks, and, of course, the obligatory coffee maker. *Maybe a strong cup of coffee will shake out the cobwebs.*

He wrapped his fingers gingerly around the steaming cup of Columbian bold brew and returned to his worktable. He pushed aside the GRM plans and took out his 18-inch by 24-inch sketchpad and started doodling. He found that if he engaged the creative side of his brain when he was stumped with some scientific or mathematical problem, things often became clearer far more quickly. The salt air was blowing across his back and brilliant rays of liquid gold were cascading across his table. The atmosphere in the building had taken on a life of its own and was infiltrating every cell of Noah's being. He hadn't felt this energetic and creative and free in, well, never. This was an exhilarating roller coaster ride and Noah wanted to flow with it to whatever the destination might be.

Soon there were pages of sketches scattered on the floor and across the table and pretty much any surface within Noah's reach. His coffee had been abandoned hours ago and shadows were now fingering their way across the room. The automatic lighting system came on noiselessly and flooded the room with a warm glow. He wasn't sure anymore if it was the lights or if there was some otherworldly luminescence surrounding him. Right now it didn't matter. He had to finish. But what was he working on exactly?

He sensed more than heard a soft rustle behind him. The scent of Hawaiian coconut mixed with exotic floral notes wafted into the room. Recognizing Sara's signature perfume, he greeted her without turning around. "Hi, honey. I'm so glad you're back."

Sara padded over behind him, her bare feet moving silently across the tile floor. She wrapped her arms around him and rested her head on his shoulder, peering past him. He could feel her damp hair, fresh from the shower, and her perfume was even more intoxicating up close. He closed his eyes and let all his senses soak in the moment. It seemed that his senses were becoming more alive each day lately. He'd never experienced this enhanced ability to absorb his surroundings like this in his life. At first, it was daunting, almost a sensory overload. But he was getting more used to it.

"What's my favorite mad scientist been up to all afternoon?" whispered Sara into his ear.

"I'm not altogether sure, Sara. I think it has something to do with a dream, or vision, or maybe just a hallucination, I had last night. It's a long story and I'm not certain that I even believe it myself yet. Before I show you what I've been working on, let's sit down over here by the windows and I'll try to explain." Noah turned and took Sara by the hand, guiding her over to sit by him on the sofa. She curled up next to him as he placed his arm around her shoulders.

"Remember last night after dinner, I said I was coming in here to pick up some papers to study before turning in?" Sara nodded against his chest without saying anything.

"I guess I was more tired than I realized and lay down on the sofa to close my eyes for a minute. The next thing I knew I was startled awake and nearly fell on the floor trying to get to my feet. I thought I heard someone calling out my name. The whole room was bathed in this brilliant glowing light and a presence permeated the space. Time stood still and I thought my heart would as well." Noah continued as the words tumbled out with hardly a breath in between.

As he recounted the entire experience, the atmosphere in the room began to change once again, like it had earlier this afternoon when he started working on his sketches. With the energy came clarity and with clarity came a conviction of the reality of his experience. He hoped his wife would find it in her heart to believe him and embrace what he was about to commit his family to.

When he finished his recounting of the events of the previous night, Sara sat quietly pressed close against him. He could feel her breathing, deep, steady breaths. He sensed she was trying to keep her grip on reality by sheer willpower. He waited for her response, unconsciously holding his own breath.

Sara unfolded from his grip and repositioned herself so she could look deeply into the eyes of the man she loved more dearly than anything. He was the father of her incredible children, a man of unquestionable character, a man to whom she had entrusted her life on more than one occasion over the years. Everything she knew to be true about her husband was in one moment being challenged to the maximum. But, above all else, she knew Noah to be a man of great faith and a man who continually pursued an intimate relationship with God. He was not a man prone to empty emotionalism when it came to his relationship with God, and he had always taught his family that if they would remain close to God, they would recognize His voice and would never be led astray. No matter what they would face, God would always be faithful to answer them and show them the truth.

This was a moment when Sara was going to have to lean on her husband's faith and conviction until hers could catch up. "Lord, help me to know your will in this situation and honor You as well as my husband," she prayed to herself before she spoke.

# CHAPTER SEVENTEEN

COMPUTER SCREENS ACROSS the globe were screaming the same headlines. Micro Global Access Connections (GAC) was streaming video across the globe as quickly as it could gain access to information. President Hy Wells' daughter, Mercury, had been in a serious one-car accident on her way to Camp David to spend the weekend with her parents. Rumors swirled across the Internet about the extent of her injuries as well as her current location.

Rionne Sanders had aced the competition and could be seen standing in the middle of a fairly deserted stretch of road near where the accident was supposed to have taken place. Secret Service personnel and the customary black SUVs were keeping prying eyes well away from the supposed accident site. Rionne's often ruthless ambition had gained her many questionable connections that provided her with inside information on any breaking story. But this one had a wall of silence so thick that it was barely possible to get anything on the air beyond conjecture. Reporting exact facts had never been an issue with the GAC and all the media subsidiaries it controlled. After all, it was about entertainment, first and foremost. So a little bend on the facts would never be noticed, only the ratings and the dividends.

"We're at the crash site where Mercury Wells, the twenty-five-year-old daughter of President Wells and his wife Marion, is said to have been critically injured just hours ago in what was reported to have been a freak one-car accident. She was travelling from a weekend in the mountains to meet her parents at their Camp David retreat when the accident is said to have occurred. The road was shrouded in unusually heavy fog for this time of year and it is speculated that she may have had difficulty seeing the road and overcorrected on one of the curves, losing control of her late model sports car and skidding off the embankment, slamming headlong into a tree. We have been prevented from taking any photos of the nearly demolished car, and it is said that the Secret Service has already had it removed from the scene for security purposes."

Rionne's practiced enthusiasm was reaching a fevered pitch as she spoke directly into the camera. This was going to be her ticket to advancement, and she planned on taking this ride as far as it would go.

"Sources have indicated that Mercury was taken by helicopter to an undisclosed medical facility in the Poconos where specialists from around the world are rumored to be gathering to attend to her medical care. Senator Nash Brookline was spending the weekend with the Wells family at Camp David when news of the accident reached the First Family. We believe that he has joined the family at the medical facility as well. We will be bringing you news updates every hour as we can gather additional information. This is Rionne Sanders signing off."

The lights clicked off and Rionne's face took on a brooding look. Something was brewing and she was determined to call in every favor she was owed to get the score on this story. She would find out what was really going on if she had to hire her own helicopters and scour the Poconos to discover this mystery medical facility. Besides, why hadn't anyone ever heard of this place before now? She was a dog with a juicy bone and no one was going to take this one away from her.

Out of radar range and beyond the coastline of the United States, Air Force One screamed across the Atlantic headed directly to Sydney. The precious cargo, Mercury Wells, was being kept alive by every newly developed piece of medical machinery that this jet aircraft could contain. The President's private physician had been in constant contact with Dr. Balfour Divino since the moment Mercury sustained her injuries. For any normal accident victim, this would have been the end. There were no options available to correct so many life-threatening injuries in one person. But, then, this was no ordinary citizen. This was the daughter of President Wells, and he would move heaven and earth and risk anything on this planet to keep his daughter alive. And his closest friend, Senator Brookline, had the means and the connections to make those dreams a reality. Life for the Wells family was about to change in a way they could not have imagined and the world was going to follow.

Unmarked vehicles waited at an uncharted landing strip outside of Sydney. The trip to Dr. Divino's facility would take less than an hour. This valuable time could have been spent praying to whatever god you believed in. But instead, strategies were carefully set in place and the entire event was being scripted down to the minutest detail. In a sense they were all praying to their own gods. They had embarked upon the ultimate arrogance. They were about to play God. And there was no turning back.

Hy and Marion Wells never were completely aware of what Dr. Balfour Divino had been working on throughout the years. They had heard rumors like everyone else about experiments that some would consider ethically questionable. But they knew better than to pry into certain areas. As a political family whose life was spent constantly in the spotlight, they learned early on the advantages of always maintaining "plausible deniability." Senator Brookline, on the other hand, maneuvered in a slightly different atmosphere. Hy had depended upon Nash for his election and was heavily relying upon Nash's successful worldwide diplomacy to get him elected to the position of Global First Citizen at the end of his current term. He owed Nash in a very big way. And he was about to owe him for the life of his daughter.

The vehicles ground to a halt before an amazing ultramodern facility constructed right into the side of a mountain of red rock formations. Trying to find it without a GPS would be nearly impossible. That was Dr. Divino's plan to maintain the secrecy of his experiments and also protect the identities of his most exclusive clients.

Hy, Marion, and Nash were quickly escorted in to an extravagantly designed and opulently appointed private office while Mercury was secreted off to the operating theater.

"President Wells, Mrs. Wells, and my old friend, Nash. I am so sorry to have to make your acquaintance due to this unfortunate circumstance." Dr. Balfour extended his hand to greet the President and his wife. Nash gave him a bear hug welcome. "Please, do not concern yourself about Mercury. Her complete medical records are on file and her condition has been monitored every moment by computer during your journey."

"Everything at the facility is at your disposal and a suite has been prepared for you and one for you as well, Nash. I hope that you will find everything to your satisfaction. I don't know how much Nash has explained to you about my work here—"

"What can you do to save my daughter? I don't really care about your accommodations. I care about Mercury." The voice of a father in pain emanated from the usually conservative and self-controlled President Wells. "Is she going to make it? Will she be able to walk? Will she still look like my beautiful daughter?" Hy and Marion were holding onto each other afraid that if either let go the other would crumble.

Sensing the mounting emotional volatility, Nash ushered them both to sit down on the plush sectional, which occupied nearly a third of Dr. Divino's office. They were too exhausted to resist Nash's comforting gesture.

"Dr. Divino, I haven't explained our special relationship to the President. I thought it best for you to do the honors," Nash gestured to Dr. Divino to take a seat near the Wells as he seated himself across from the grief-stricken family and their new doctor. He casually helped himself to a cut crystal goblet of local mineral water as Dr. Divino began his explanation.

"President Wells, Mrs. Wells." He smiled at the couple and they barely managed to nod in agreement. "You have probably heard of my experiments, which produced the artificial womb for the purpose of cloning a human and for which I was awarded the Crystal Flame award several years ago."

"What has this got to do with my family and my daughter's life?" Hy practically spit the words at Dr. Divino in his exasperation at the way this entire scene seemed to be moving in slow motion.

"Patience, patience. I understand your concerns. I developed a means by which sufficient DNA could be extracted from any person, and, using my proprietary methods of nourishment and life support, a complete, healthy, and *exact* replication of that individual could be "born" at the appropriate time. We have had many success stories over the years and many very grateful individuals. These successes have allowed me to perfect this process beyond where anyone dared go before." Dr. Divino relished this slow disclosure of his accomplishments.

"You see, I have some clients that have expressed concerns about both insuring and maintaining their continued health in the face of certain unavoidable dangers. Some are concerned about contracting a terminal disease, which would require major organ replacement. Some live such dangerous or daring lives that they are concerned about sustaining life-threatening injuries from which they might not recover fully. Others merely have so much wealth that their only concern is to remain appearing as if they had discovered their own personal Fountain of Youth. And in a way, I suppose one could look at this situation in that way." Dr. Divino paused.

"Please, Dr. Divino. Get to the point." Hy's self-control was eroding, and he was fighting like a drowning man to maintain some shred of it. "Where are you going with all this, and what does it have to do with me and my family? I've never even met you in person before this very moment. How does all this matter to me right now?"

"Hy. May I call you that? Some years ago, when you were elected to office, your friend Nash brought me several samples of DNA for a specific purpose. He had arranged that when each of your family members underwent your normal physical examinations, a sample of your DNA was extracted under my specific instructions. Those DNA samples were brought here to my laboratory and placed inside my newly designed artificial living environment pods. You see, I have perfected the artificial womb to go far beyond the gestation period which would normally bring forth a bounding, healthy baby after nine months." Dr. Divino's smile looked more like a leering reptile about to pounce upon its prey. His hooded eyes flashed from a deep Mediterranean blue to midnight black in an instant. Emptiness and icy cold were exposed momentarily and gone again.

Hy and Marion felt the breath being sucked out of their lungs at the prospect of what Dr. Divino was about to unveil. At this moment everything in Hy's soul screamed for the safety shield of a life of "plausible deniability." He was on a cold dark precipice and was about to be plunged over the edge.

Dr. Divino continued his explanation with a rapid tone. "I have developed a method which allows the cloned fetus to remain in stasis, unconscious indefinitely. It will still continue to develop until it has reached a state equivalent to that of an adult body. At that time it will remain in a maintenance mode until the donor has need of an organ or a bone or fairly any part of the "second self," as we like to call them. I have given donors a limitless extension of life and health. I, and I alone, can give your daughter life." He paused dramatically to allow the weight of his words to sink deep into the Wells' consciousness.

He wanted them to know exactly how much power he was wielding and how much power was being offered them. He held their daughter's life in his hands. Even while he was disclosing this scenario, specially trained surgeons were replacing Mercury's injured and irreparably damaged organs and bones with those of her unique second self. When they finished, no one would ever know how close to death she had been. There would be no evidence of the extremity of her injuries. There would be no chance of organ or tissue rejection. Her recovery would appear to be miraculous. Even she would never know what procedures she had undergone. It would all be managed like every other news event. The happy family would pose together once more. The emotional duress of the Wells family would only serve to endear them more to the public and the unmistakable devotion of their family friend, Nash Brookline, would cement his place in their future forever.

Marion squeezed Hy's arm so tightly he thought she was going to stop the flow of blood. He had sold his soul for his career years ago, as a young politician scrambling up the ladder of success. He hadn't cared what the price would be at that time. He had been willing to pay it. Now he knew the enormity of the price he had agreed to pay. It was a bitter taste. He looked at Nash again. What Nash and Divino were now offering was beyond his wildest dreams. The power he would be able to access was limitless. Power and control. The twin aphrodisiacs. The taste was slowly sweetening.

# CHAPTER EIGHTEEN

B EFORE SARA COULD speak, Noah reached over and took
her delicate face in his hands. Looking deeply into her
beautiful brown eyes, he tried to keep his voice from
quavering as he saw a single tear tracing its way down her cheek.
As he gently wiped away the tear, he found himself experiencing
that overwhelming love that he'd had for Sara on his wedding day
many years ago. He knew in his heart that God had brought them
together and he had to depend on that kernel of faith to keep them
united in whatever this adventure was that was unfolding before
them.

"Sara, I know how hard it is for you to understand, let alone
believe, all that I have shared with you this evening. I've experienced it and I am still having difficulty wrapping my mind around
the ramifications of all this, for us, for our family..." he hesitated,
"for the world."

She reached up and placed her hands gently over his. "Noah,
I believe you. I don't understand any of it. But I trust you. And,
more importantly, I trust our God. If He has given you this
mission; if He has made the decisions that you say He has, then He
is big enough to confirm all this to me and to each of our children
and their wives. I'm going to pray that He reveals this visit and
His mission to each of them tonight in their dreams. We'll know
soon enough when we all gather together for breakfast tomorrow.
In the meantime, show me what you've been working on all day.

The place looks like someone threw a bomb in a paper factory."
She playfully pulled Noah to his feet, and they walked over to the
worktable hand in hand.

Noah was grateful for the momentary break from the seri-
ousness of their conversation. But what he was about to show
Sara was nothing that she could imagine either. He gathered all
the pages of sketches together and placed them atop one another
so they were in order. He turned over one page after another.
Each page had intricate designs complete with dimensions and
instructions for assembly. The last page made all the previous
ones make sense.

On the very last page was a detailed drawing of what appeared
to be a huge ship, fairly square, with a roof and a door on the
side. The proportions were enormous, but explained all the floor
plans and minute sections depicted in the previous pages. Sara
gasped. It was real. Just like the dream or vision or whatever it
was that Noah had experienced. Somehow, the plans for this ship
had been downloaded into Noah's mind and transferred onto
paper in a very short period of time. She knew enough about
building and planning to know it was not humanly possible
for all this work to have been accomplished from inception to
working drawings so quickly and with such detail and accuracy.
Even as talented as Noah was, this was definitely not his area of
expertise.

Nevertheless, here they were, in front of her. She clasped Noah's
hand more tightly. Where there had been confusion and doubt,
peace was ebbing in and pushing all other thoughts aside. She
welcomed this supernatural peace much like a person dying of
thirst welcomes a cool drink of water.

Now to see what would be revealed in the morning.

"Noah, you always promised me that our life together would

never be dull. You said that you couldn't promise riches, but that we would always have adventure. I guess you meant it." They held tightly to one another and breathed in the cool night air. Yes, tomorrow would be very illuminating and life altering for the entire family.

# Chapter Nineteen

Imposing thunderheads cleared lazily, allowing the African skies over the Rift Valley to open to the brilliant downpour of mid-afternoon sunlight. Huge, almost primitive looking barges were making their way effortlessly down the Congo River, eventually to be unloaded and transferred to the local railway system for transport across the Atlantic.

The nearly three thousand miles of the River Congo make it the second longest river in Africa and its unique location allows it to transverse the second largest rainforest area in the world. The river's westward flow is steady as it winds it way towards the deep canyons and cataracts that form just before Livingstone Falls. That's where the railway system that bypasses the falls picks up all cargo heading for the ocean.

Months of bloodshed between the feuding tribal leaders of the newly birthed country of Kongolasa had finally given way to an uneasy truce. The leaders of the ruling tribe had destroyed the long held sacred stand of gopher wood trees to make way for land and mineral dealings with the much wealthier surrounding countries. The disputing tribal leaders were enraged at the destruction. Their pain and anguish at the irrevocable loss could not be assuaged even in light of the leaders' offer to use the gopher wood to build a palace for the newly elected ruling party.

At a most critical point, where generational pride was beginning to dissolve reason, diplomacy intervened and an ambassador from the United States accompanied by Senator Nash Brookline arrived on the scene. They managed to broker a very profitable deal to acquire the roughly hewn timber and have it shipped to the United States as well as negotiate a very advantageous contract with the neighboring countries for oil and mineral rights. Everyone saved face. And soon, even this tiny newly formed country might very well be the site of yet another Teen Express in the future.

All this had taken place months ago. The barges had long since divested themselves of their precious cargo. And huge containers from the Rift Valley could now be seen being off-loaded at the port of San Diego. Their destination neatly and boldly stenciled across the sides: Biosphere Five, California, United States.

# CHAPTER TWENTY

NOAH REACHED OVER to his nightstand to shut off the offending alarm screech before turning over for a few more precious minutes of sleep.

The sound interrupted his sleep again.

"What's wrong with this alarm clock?" Noah mumbled as he tried in vain to rub the sleep from his eyes. Before the intruding noise offended his senses one more time and possibly woke up Sara, he finally realized that the offender was his cell phone which was now precariously perched on the edge of the nightstand ready to launch itself into space. He managed to grab the phone and flip it open before the inevitable.

"Arcmann here," he gruffed into the phone.

"Noah, my good man. How are things in beautiful, sunny Southern California this gorgeous afternoon? Oh, I mean, it must be pretty early in the day for you on that Coast." The voice on the other end of the line laughed at his own attempt at humor.

"Senator Brookline. Good morning. I'm surprised to hear from you so soon."

"I apologize for the early call, but my constituents and I are very eager to hear some good news about our pet project. Biosphere Five has not been on the newslines or GAC nearly enough to generate a sufficient revenue stream lately. I wanted to find out your team's appraisal of the situation." Senator Brookline's New England accent turned slightly rapier at the end, Noah thought.

"Well, we just assembled our entire family, err, I mean team, and have done some cursory investigating thus far. Our initial appraisal seems to indicate that Biosphere Five is severely under-sized and under-equipped in materials, supplies, and staff. At the rate that new pairs of animals and plants are arriving from every continent on the globe, we'll need to temporarily build outdoor habitats for holding areas while we re-design the structures that would be necessary for the project to achieve the results that your consortium promised." Noah hesitated as the weight of his brief commentary drifted into Senator Brookline's thoughts.

"Dr. Arcmann," Senator Brookline's voice changed drastically in tenor as he responded. "I realize that as a member of outstanding reputation in the scientific community, you may not be familiar with the intricacies of politics and diplomacy. In fact, that's an admirable quality. Why not leave all those nasty jobs to those who excel in those areas anyway?" Brookline continued in a most measured and stern tone, almost as if he was sharing a deep secret with a hidden threat attached.

"The President and I and several other world leaders have committed to the results of this project to instill a sense of vision and trust in the world about the condition of our environment. We know that there are some legitimate concerns about such things as species extinction and depletion of nourishment for certain animal and plant life due to our ever-expanding popula-tion and industrial development. But," he paused, "these concerns are minor compared to the global balance of power and the deli-cate diplomacy necessary to ensure world peace for yet another generation. I'm certain that you agree so far, Noah." He continued without pausing for an answer from a puzzled Noah.

"In the end we need results to satisfy both our current donors as well as future donors from the world markets. In order to sustain this and maintain the trust of the world community, we need some visuals that will convey the idea of industrious progress and visionary planning for the future. That's where you and your team come in, Noah." Brookline was now oozing with practiced diplomacy.

"We are getting requests for receipt of more species every day. And we need to give this project another financial transfusion immediately. I need results and the results I need immediately are those that will ensure a top spot on the evening news for the next month. Are you with me, Noah?"

"Senator, I'm not certain I understand what you would consider newsworthy action on our part right now."

"All I want from you is a few press conferences highlighting the daily arrivals of new animals and plant specimens. Some detailed footage of construction of additional habitats. You know, that sort of thing. And color it with as much scientific jargon as you can to hold the audience's attention and open their checkbooks. And, Noah, you have every piece of equipment and any supplies you need at your immediate disposal. In fact, I heard that some rare gopher wood lumber has just arrived at the site. Help yourself to as much of that as you need for anything. Anything at all. I want plenty of coverage of our using that special donation from Kongalasa. That would make a great news story, right there." Before Noah could respond or gather his thoughts, the Senator bid him farewell and assured him that he would always be available to Noah for any consultation or brainstorming session. As abruptly as this morning intrusion occurred, it was terminated, leaving Noah to puzzle out the meaning of all that had just transpired. He could not linger too long on this conversation because he remembered that this was the morning Sara had set up for the litmus test of what he had revealed to her the previous evening. This was going to be some earth-shattering morning for the Arcmann clan.

While he had been on the phone with Senator Brookline, Sara had awakened, dressed, and gone into the kitchen to fix coffee and start breakfast for the family. Noah decided a quick shower was definitely in order. Maybe some cool water would clear his brain and his spirit and help him prepare for what he was about to address. He uttered a desperate distress prayer as he finished dressing and headed into the kitchen.

He was more than a little surprised to see the entire family, dressed and fixing breakfast and setting the table. Everyone moved with precision, but silently, completely lost in their own worlds of thought. Noah thought it best not to break the flow, so he sat down, led everyone in muttering a version of blessing over the food, and dug in. Breakfast passed quickly, and then, as if on cue, Noah found all seven sets of eyes turned toward him for the next move.

Noah cleared his throat nervously.

"Your Mom and I were wondering if any of you had any dreams or anything last night?"

One could almost hear blood pressures rising and pulses quickening. As if a dam had been broken, all three boys and their brides began to share almost identical stories. Each had witnessed a scene that replayed the vision or, more appropriately, the visitation that Noah had experienced. Even Sara added her own version of the dream to that of her sons and their wives.

"Noah, I think it's time for you to explain to our family what you explained to me last night. Family, listen with your ears and your hearts to what your father is about to share. And pray as you listen that the Lord will confirm in your heart the truth and conviction of what you have all experienced." Sara nodded the floor to Noah.

Noah began to *feel* more than see that brilliant mist filling the entire room and enveloping each member of his family still gathered around the breakfast table. It seemed to grow and diffuse and then permeate every fiber of their being. He wondered if each of them were sharing this part of the experience at the same moment. Strengthened and encouraged, Noah started his story.

He explained how over the last year he had been having these extraordinary dreams that he thought were just the result of an overactive imagination. He tried to discount them, but could never quite shake the intensity of the experience. Each of the dreams had been some version of a cataclysmic event that appeared to bring on worldwide devastation. He shared some details from each of the dreams to give his family a sense of the monumental proportions of this looming catastrophe. He shared that the dreams had escalated in frequency and intensity and had finally culminated in what he now affirmed in his heart was a divine visitation and commissioning for himself and his entire family.

As crazy as it sounded, God had spoken and directed Noah and his family to build a ship of very specific proportions and to gather two of each animal type and prepare for an impending flood which would wipe out every living thing.

"The purposes of God are known only fully to Him. But the truth of His words is engraved on my heart. And I hope, after hearing what I have shared and after experiencing what you have all experienced last night, you will agree with God's directive and we can work together to complete this ship as quickly as possible." Noah paused to allow the weight of his words to rest upon his family.

"I know that as I have been speaking to you, each of you has been silently praying for some confirmation personal to you."

"Have you received affirmation and a conviction in your hearts?" Noah made eye contact with each person sitting at the table. Each pair of eyes was moist as tears streamed down many faces. Each person shook his or her head with determination and a solemnity that he had never witnessed before. This was a holy moment for the Arcmann family. The adventure had begun and the clock was ticking.

# CHAPTER TWENTY-ONE

R IONNE SANDERS' FACE filled the screen as she breathlessly
began her coverage of the two main stories that had occupied the newslines recently. Amid a cacophony of snapping
cameras and dozens of microphones, President Hy Wells, his
wife Marion, and Nash Brookline intertwined their arms around
the President's daughter, Mercury. They were all smiles and the
beaming poster children for health and power.

"Amid global speculation and rumor, Mercury Wells has
returned from her brief stay at the undisclosed medical facility in
the nearby mountains looking none the worse for wear. As many
of you are aware, Mercury suffered a life-threatening accident a
little over a month ago. There ensued worldwide concerns over her
ability not only to survive the unfortunate and freak accident, but
whether she would be fully functional. As if by some miracle of
modern science, or as Senator Brookline shared, by sheer Wells
family guts and determination, you see before you Mercury Wells
looking more vibrant and full of energy than ever before," Rionne
gushed to the camera.

"The family has declined any personal interviews stating that
this is a personal family matter and that they want to preserve the
privacy of their daughter. They would only offer their sincere and
heartfelt appreciation for a world of well-wishers and attributed
the unity of thought that surrounded their daughter's recupera-
tion for her amazing results. They also indicated that the best

tribute they could offer the world is to rededicate themselves even more passionately to the purposes of world peace and scientific supremacy. So, there you have the very latest on the First Family." Rionne signed off only to reappear immediately on the second story of world interest.

"Rionne Sanders here just outside the family compound of Drs. Noah and Sara Arcmann in Southern California. As you know, there has been a great deal of unexplained activity on the Arcmann property in the last month. While we have been able to interview Dr. Noah Arcmann on numerous occasions about the work that he and his incredibly talented family have been doing on behalf of the Biosphere Five Project, he had been extremely close-mouthed regarding the speculation on the work that has been going on at the farthest point on his personal property." Rionne's eyes gleamed with the richness of the potential in this story.

"In recent months, there has been much speculation regarding the viability of the Biosphere Five Project which has been supported and promoted by President Hy Wells and Senator Nash Brookline. Seemingly every nation on the globe has been experiencing severe shortages of plant life as well and potential extinction of some animal types. Once Biosphere Five was presented to the world, the donations of plants and animals became almost overwhelming.

"The underwriters of the Biosphere finally felt it necessary to call in the top experts in the various fields affected to take over the directorship of the Biosphere and bring about the results that the world has been waiting for. Dr. Noah Arcmann and his wife, noted scientist Dr. Sara Arcmann, were called in to take over director-ship of the Biosphere Five. They, along with their three sons, each holding a doctorate in his own field of related expertise, have been working at a fevered pace lately." Rionne nodded attention to a clip of a previous interview.

"In a taped interview earlier this month, Dr. Arcmann, when

asked about the goals for Biosphere Five, offered these enigmatic words." Rionne had the station switch to the tape.

"Dr. Arcmann, do you feel that there is really any urgency in completing the work of the Biosphere? And, if so, what can you tell us about it?"

"Rionne, I wish I could explain thoroughly why there is such a sense of urgency over the success of this project. But all I can offer is that catastrophic events are about to unfold in nature which will bring untold destruction upon the globe. You may have noted that the stories of tsunamis are increasing in frequency and severity." Noah continued with a grave look in his eyes.

"Increasing movement in tectonic plates, which have remained virtually silent for centuries, has been detected all over the world. Extreme weather patterns have been forming at an alarming rate. Storm cells are forming and re-forming over every landmass, threatening deluge of unforeseen proportions. It's as if the earth is groaning in preparation for an enormous alteration." Noah paused as he seemed to contemplate the prophetic weight of his own words.

"Dr. Arcmann, there have been rumors that the pressure of the responsibility of directorship of this project has had some ill effects on you and your family. Speculation has arisen among the scientific community that you have begun to see demons around every corner and are perhaps becoming a little paranoid; that maybe you're convinced that all these signs are indicators that for some reason the end of the world is imminent." Rionne chuckled at the last statement to Noah, as if challenging him to rebuke her.

"I can only follow the dictates of my beliefs. As a scientist, I can tell you that there are irrefutable indicators that a planetary shift is about to occur. Whatever paradigm through which you interpret scientific evidence, you must come to the same conclusions. There is indeed a disastrous change approaching, and life as we know it will never be the same. Now, if you don't mind, I have to get back to my work. Thank you for your time, Miss Sanders."

"One more thing, Dr. Arcmann. Is it true that in addition to your work at Biosphere Five, you are building some sort of enormous ship on your property? Do you think that somehow you can ensure the safety of your family in this imagined catastrophe? What good do you think can possibly come from such a ridiculous project? Are you sure that your objectivity isn't being tainted by such fanatical ideas? May we come to your compound and photograph the Arcmann, what shall we call it, the Arcmann Ark?"

Rionne's eyes glinted into the glaring lights from the nearby cameras following her and Noah out of the studio. Noah walked with determination and she matched him step for step. When the camera zoomed in for the last face shot before she signed off, her azure eyes slitted, inky black, and then returned to azure. She had captured her prey and turned this interview to her advantage. This story might very well be her ticket to worldwide recognition and then she truly could control her own destiny. So what if it destroyed the credibility of a fine family in the process. Ratings, entertainment, that's all that mattered. And this was entertainment and reality programming at its finest. If Romie Rogers was unable to get an on-screen guest appearance with Dr. Noah Arcmann and his brilliant wife Dr. Sara Arcmann, maybe she, Rionne Sanders, could find a way to get herself invited on the show and spin her own web of intrigue to the audience about this ridiculous family and their notions of worldwide destruction. She was licking her lips in anticipation. This would be juicy. Spilled blood usually was.

# CHAPTER TWENTY-TWO

J AKE AND HAM nudged one of the last floor joists into place on the upper deck of the Arcmann Ark. The newslines were tagging the ship *Arcmann's Folly* among other titles. The family had settled simply upon the "Ark." It seemed short and to the point.

Something smelled delicious. Shem approached with an armload of sandwiches and cold bottles of water. "Anybody up here hungry?" Shem tossed a sandwich to each of his brothers. They all settled down on the floor and leaned against the sturdy sides of the ship to eat lunch.

The smell of freshly cut gopher wood was still a pretty heady aroma. And mixed with the sweet smell of tantalizing roast beef sandwiches with the works, the way Shem always prepared them for the brothers, the scent made each of them relax and enjoy the moment.

"I can't get over how quickly and cleanly this ship has come together," Jake offered, his mouth filled with meat. The others nodded in agreement. Each had at some time or other in their travels been involved in construction; some complex and some fairly primitive. They could all comprehend the complexity of this project and so it was that they appreciated the almost otherworldly synergy that seemed to permeate each task.

"Dad wants us to let him know when this upper level is finished so he can make an inspection and re-evaluate the time schedule." Ham craned his neck to look around the substantial breadth of this upper deck.

Every aspect of this ship was unique and interlaced with a precision that outshone anything that science or technology could provide. Yet it all seemed so simple in its design and construction, minimalism at its finest. The ship was supposed to house two of every animal type along with provisions for the animals and the Arcmann families. There were somewhat Spartan living quarters for each of the four families at one end of the top deck above the three levels that comprised the hold of the ship. Access to the outside deck was available only through a single passageway bisecting the living quarters.

The skylights, interspersed throughout the roof of the ship, provided more than adequate lighting for the living quarters as well as sufficient lighting for the lower decks. There was a passageway leading from the living quarters to the lower decks for provision and for tending to the animals that would be in their care. They were becoming more confident in their ability to finish this project in time and to provide for the care of the animals entrusted to them as Noah continued to share new bits and pieces of revelation that were given to him each day.

"The animals at the Biosphere are becoming more and more agitated every day. I think they are aware that something is coming." Ham wiped the crumbs from his mouth as he finished his sandwich.

"I imagine that once we have been given the go ahead, it shouldn't be too much trouble to herd the animals from the Biosphere through the forest area and into the Ark." Ham looked closely at his brothers. "It would be so much easier if there was a straight shot from the Biosphere to the Ark, but we don't have time to carve out a road through the forest. I also think that somehow the natural tendencies of all these animals may be altering already so that they will feel at ease in close proximity to one another."

"I've noticed a change in them too. It's as if they are finding some kind of temporary comfort in the proximity of unfamiliar animals. Almost like coming together against a common enemy makes what were once deadly enemies suddenly friends." Jake seemed proud of his evaluation of the unfolding situation.

"Dad thinks that once all the animals have been boarded, they will enter into a state of hibernation which will last until it is determined to be safe to disembark. He said it would require far less nourishment and less care and would make the passage more peaceful in the end." Jake was letting his mounting excitement show in front of his brothers.

"As terrifying as the prospect of what lies ahead may seem, I'm almost looking forward to this adventure moving into full swing."

"Why do you say that?" questioned Shem, polishing off the last of his bottled water.

"It's been so very difficult on Mom and Dad these last months. They have always taken their work seriously and been well respected by anyone who knew anything about science. And since we have begun building this ship, they have been ridiculed and barely tolerated by their peers. The media coverage has been brutal and even the President and his buddy Brookline have begun to make subtle and not-so-subtle threats against Mom and Dad. If it weren't for the ban over the airspace above Biosphere Five that Brookline initiated a year ago to ensure his complete control over the media coverage, we would be inundated with reporters and helicopters day and night." Jake shook his head. The thoughts of all that had happened recently overwhelmed him.

"The Arcmann name is now a household word. Maybe household

*joke* is more accurate," added Shem. "In some ways, I guess the isolation that this has caused the family may have worked to our ultimate advantage in the long run."

"All I know is that I am so proud of our wives. They have been strong and comforting and encouraging throughout this entire process," beamed Ham. "I'm glad they have each other to confide in. They really have become more like sisters than sisters-in-law, haven't they, guys?"

Somehow the girls had managed to find ways of acquiring all the supplies needed, from daily foodstuffs for the family, to extraordinary wood tools or other building supplies that the guys needed for the ship. They had figured out which furnishings, though minimal, would provide the most use in their limited space. They designed the storage areas for maximum utility in storing all the food and water supplies that would be needed for the adventure. They acquired everything necessary to start over again from scratch. They were determined to rise to this challenge and truly partner with their husbands in the completion of this great ship. They were, all eight family members, of one mind in this; the first of many miracles that would surround the building of this Ark. Many, many miracles would follow. Sometimes it was good not to know too much in advance. "Just enough for today" had become the Arcmann motto. And it was working just fine.

# CHAPTER TWENTY-THREE

NOAH WAS WRESTED from his uneasy sleep by the sound of wind whipping against the house. He could hear rain pattering against the wall of windows in the master bedroom. The smell of freshly falling rain, tinged with salt air, the rhythmic symphony of the raindrops against the glass, would normally have made him pull the warm, oversized down comforter around his ears and allow himself to melt beneath its weight as he snuggled next to Sara. As if on cue, Sara turned over and curled up next to him and settled in for a few more moments of sleep. But today, Noah couldn't find the usual comfort in their snuggling. He gently extricated himself from the covers without disturbing Sara. As he gazed down on her peaceful, almost angelic face, he reminded himself of how incredibly lucky he was to have her for his wife. She was indeed his partner in life and now his partner for the greatest adventure in the world. Many times he felt he might not be able to hold the reins steady for his family during this work. But every time he began to waiver, Sara would come alongside him and remind him of where his strength truly emanated from. She encouraged him to stop whatever project he was overseeing and retreat to his office and spend some time meditating on the Scriptures and praying for guidance.

She was also sharing this encouragement with Shem, Ham, and Jake and especially with their wives. She was the anchor for the family and also its greatest cheerleader. And, best of all, she followed her own advice for more hours than Noah could count. He had awakened many a night lately to find Sara's side of the bed empty and eventually find her curled up in her office, Bible open on her lap and eyes closed in contemplation, a look of peace emanating from her beautiful face. He wouldn't disturb her at those moments, because he knew she was strengthening herself for whatever challenge would arise and also was interceding for him. Yes, he was truly a lucky man. But was he the right man for this undertaking? He couldn't allow his thoughts to wonder at the wisdom of God's choice of his family. It led nowhere and leeched energy and resolve. He had faith and conviction. God would provide the rest.

Right now, he needed to get outside and take a look at the skies and check the weather bulletins on the Internet in his office; then some much needed meditation and asking for guidance and time frames for what would come next.

Noah didn't bother to put on a rain jacket to walk over to his office building. Even as a young boy he had always enjoyed the freedom of walking through the rain. There was something freeing and invigorating about being outside during a storm and allowing the rain to soak him to the skin. Maybe it was the heightened ozone content that made the plants green up after a good rain, or maybe it was just the perennial little boy in him, but it always felt good and today would be no exception. As he made his way across the rain-soaked grass to their office, he glanced up through the trees at the far end of their property. If he looked closely he could just barely make out the outline of the Ark standing proudly amid the little section of undeclared national forest that formed the outside boundary of their property. He squeezed his eyes shut and opened them again. Was he imagining it or did it appear that the Ark had a glow emanating from it? Maybe the rain and ground fog was just playing tricks on him. He made a mental note to go over to the Ark after breakfast and check it out. Now, for more important endeavors.

He entered his office, flicked on the lights, and immediately made a pot of coffee. As it brewed, he turned on the computer and checked all the weather stations across the globe for news that had occurred overnight. Each website he visited confirmed what he had feared. Thunderstorms had moved across every continent. Steady rainfall was being reported. They concurred this was nothing to worry about. But what no one seemed to be noticing was that it was steady everywhere on the globe. *It was beginning.*

By the time Noah finished in his office and went back to the house, breakfast was on the table and the family joined hands and prayed to start their day.

"Did anyone check the weather bulletins yet?" Jake inquired as he shoveled eggs and bacon onto his plate.

"I checked my laptop when I got up and it looks as though the storm fronts are beginning to join together. I didn't get a chance to check the geologic reports yet, though," added Ham between bites of buttermilk biscuit.

"I checked them both this morning and activity is increasing dramatically. I think we need to start loading the Ark with all the provisions and water. And as soon as we are finished we need to start over to the Biosphere and begin herding the animals over here," Noah smiled. "We won't know exactly what to expect until we actually start moving them. But I suspect that somehow we will be amazed once again."

He had gotten used to sharing these times together with his family. He had always been proud of them and relished the events that brought them together in the past. But this experience had brought their family interdependency and respect for one another to a whole new level. He could never have imagined a family could work together in such complete unity and with such joy and self-sacrifice. If he ever had any doubts about God's hand in this entire endeavor, the peace and joy that his family was experiencing dispelled them completely. Today was a good day. *We should rejoice in it!*

# CHAPTER TWENTY-FOUR

A s the girls finished clearing away breakfast, Sara joined Ham and Shem in preparing the supplies to be transported to the Ark. They had used their electric trucks, each equipped with a hitch to attach a modest sized utility trailer, to move the smaller supplies around the property and to get quickly back and forth from the Ark site. All the supplies had been wrapped and sealed in waterproof containers, compact enough for ease of transport and storage once aboard the ship.

Jake had already taken one of the electric trucks filled with a load of pitch to place some finishing touches on the exterior of the ship. They had successfully managed to seal the entire exterior body of the Ark with a special blend of pitch that had been revealed to Noah. This special blend would act as incredible waterproofing as well as extra insulation. It may have appeared somewhat primitive to a casual observer, but Noah and the family had complete confidence in the strength of the material in concert with the manner in which they had been instructed to build the Ark from the beginning. Survival would depend on the seaworthiness of this one-of-a-kind craft.

Jake arrived at the Ark, climbed to the top deck and began doing his touchup on some of the seams near the door. Sara, Ham, and Shem pulled up to unload their trucks shortly thereafter. The rain had turned to a light sprinkle. Jake wasn't wearing any raingear. Like his Dad, he much preferred to experience the rain rather than repel it. Suddenly he noticed a strong smell in the air, the familiar smell of ozone, which generally preceded lightning strikes. The hair on his arms stood straight up. Before he could warn Sara and his brothers to take cover, he heard the ear-shattering thunder clap and saw a blinding flash of lightning. At least he thought it was lightning, but it didn't seem to stop immediately. He crawled around to the edge of the deck, peering over the side of the ship in the direction of the Biosphere. His jaw dropped in disbelief at what he was witnessing. He'd read stories about this phenomenon but credible accounts were rare and still in dispute. As he stared across the forest that separated the Ark from the Biosphere property, he witnessed a huge, fiery sphere of light, descending from the sky and then driving right through the forest in a straight line towards the Ark. The ball was at least twenty feet in diameter and trees disintegrated upon contact as the ball of fiery fury raced toward him. Jake had a front row seat to what had been best described in history books as *ball lightning*. But this exceeded any report he had ever read about and he feared that he, his family, and the Ark would be its next victims.

As suddenly as it had appeared, it reared up within yards of the Ark, shot straight upward, and disappeared into the heavens. A trail of smoke, or perhaps steam rising from the smoldering area, was left behind. The ground it had just seared was now a trough of plowed, steaming dirt much like what you might expect if a meteor had collided with the earth. But there was definitely no meteor that remained, and no meteor that created this.

"Jake! Jake! Sara! Ham! Shem! Are you all alright?" Jake heard the concern in his father's voice.

"We're fine, Noah. We're OK." Sara yelled from the doorway to the Ark. She ran to meet him.

"Dad, did you see that? What was that?" Jake was already down on the ground next to Noah, breathless from the excitement.

"From what I could tell, it appeared to be a form of ball lightning. But I thought that was just a myth. I know there were some sightings starting in 1868 and maybe a dozen others over the decades. But still there seemed to be so many alternative explanations, I was never sure." Jake placed his arm around Noah's shoulder. "I watched it form from the sky into a ball and crash through the trees and then disappear. I was certain that it was about to destroy the Ark." Noah's voice quavered. "And kill all of you."

Jake and Noah stood silently for a moment. Sara tucked herself more tightly beneath Noah's other arm as they looked out across this newly created pathway.

Ham came running towards them, his words a mixture of enthusiasm and shock. "I just went over to the trough and checked it out. It's just amazing! It's like that ball thing formed a paved highway for us directly from the Biosphere property to the front of the Ark. It's just amazing!"

"Noah," Sara turned her face up to look in his eyes. "I don't know about you, but it seems that we now have our very own transport corridor to make herding all the animals over here much, much easier. I've never heard of anything like this ever happening, but it couldn't have happened at a more opportune time for us."

"Whatever we just witnessed," offered Shem, "we should just be grateful that we are all safe and we better take advantage of any time this will save us. I have a feeling that things are going to start accelerating."

"And, I think we will be seeing more and more unexplainable occurrences as well," added Noah shaking his head in concern.

Each member of the Arcmann family continued to ruminate

over the morning's events as they finished with their plans to load the Ark with supplies in preparation for moving the animals. If all went well, they should be able to begin herding in the next few days. Tonight would be a very special night for the family as they prepared for their adventure of a lifetime. The rest of the day passed quietly, with everyone lost in their thoughts, grateful to be busy with their assigned tasks.

# CHAPTER TWENTY-FIVE

RIONNE SANDERS HAD never looked worse on camera, nor felt more exhilarated. She was huddled on the boardwalk under a huge studio umbrella with the Atlantic Ocean threatening behind her. It wasn't so much wind gusts that were making it so difficult for her to maintain her balance as it was the sheer force of the torrential rain coming down. The noise from the rain hitting the sidewalk and the top of her umbrella was making the sound crew cringe, trying to modulate the transmission so that she could be heard clearly over the airwaves.

"This is Rionne Sanders coming to you from the blustery beaches of Miami," she screamed into the microphone. "As you can see, my crew and I are the only reporting team brave enough to bring you the unfolding story as it happens once again." As she continued to speak, the camera took a slow, albeit shaky, panoramic shot of the surrounding area, settling on a view directly behind Rionne and slightly to the south.

"Behind me you can clearly distinguish the outline and shape of what can only be described as a giant column of focused rain unlike anything that anyone has ever seen before. These columns of torrential rain have been appearing randomly across the globe. Scientists cannot provide any adequate explanation of this phenomenon. They have determined that they are not twisters or miniature hurricanes or funnel clouds in any traditional sense."

Rionne paused to catch her breath and to turn to stare at the watery monster hovering just a little less than a mile off shore.

"President Wells is in the Oval Office and is about to make a statement. Let's cut to Washington DC."

"Citizens of the United States and the world, good evening." President Wells appeared in perfect harmony with his surroundings and displayed a well-practiced appearance of confidence and self-control. "By now I am certain that you have become aware of some weather anomalies being experienced across the globe. Ever since these aberrations first appeared, I have been in close contact with every experienced weather expert and scientist acquainted with this field. I have given them carte blanche to use our top research facilities in the United States as they combine their considerable knowledge to unravel the mystery of these columns of water. I have been assured by the experts that this is a once-in-a-lifetime event and certainly nothing to become overly concerned about." He managed a calming smile to the camera lens.

"Thus far, the events have only taken place over larger bodies of water, with some over lakes and a few rivers. Nothing has transpired over land and our experts assure us that we have nothing at all to worry about in that regard. We will continue to monitor any further occurrences and report our findings to you as they might develop." He paused and refocused his smile with a more piercing stare into the camera. In a moment, the smile disappeared from his eyes and a black void appeared, flitted to and fro, and immediately dissolved again. "I would like to take this opportunity to encourage all of you to search your hearts at a time like this and consider who you would feel most secure with holding the office of Global First Citizen. The United States is standing on the precipice of a new global economy, a united global scientific community, and a financial prosperity that will be unparalleled in history. This opportunity can only materialize as our country comes into unity with the Global Alliance of States and supports the election process which will occur in just a few months. I can promise you that once elected to this most prestigious position, I will be even better equipped to drive our world into a new millennium of peace and tranquility."

The Oval Office scene dissolved back to Rionne trying to stand upright on the boardwalk. "That was our President Hy Wells, assuring our country and all those viewers around the world that we have nothing to fear from a few rogue rain clouds. President Wells also took this opportunity to remind the American voting public that he is the front-runner for the position of Global First Citizen and would greatly appreciate a landslide of support from his own country. During his years in office as President, he has almost single-handedly brought about more political and economic reform that any other president in the history of this country. And the opportunities he has provided for expansion and underwriting of the scientific community locally and around the world are certainly unparalleled as well."

Rionne suddenly noticed she was shouting for no reason. She turned to look out over the ocean to where the thunderous column of water had been moments before. As if some mythic rain god had waved a magic wand, the column of water dissolved into a fine mist gently cascading upon the waves and then disappeared. She had heard of these sudden appearances and disappearances but had never personally witnessed one until now. She caught herself, mouth agape, staring over the waves. Regaining her composure, she briskly turned back to face the camera.

Eyes alight with the excitement of the shoot, she continued as if nothing abnormal had happened. "You saw it live, the dreaded column appeared, roared its mighty roar, and disappeared like a kitten. President Wells was correct. While this may seem unusual and lack any ready explanation, we have nothing to be concerned about today. This is Rionne Sanders, keeping my eyes to the skies for you."

She smiled her signature smile and the lights went black. Rionne leaped for joy after this clip was over. She knew that on every GAC news line around the globe, it was her face and her name associated with the exclusives that had been nearly avalanching into her lap. She ran back into the mobile news van to catch her other breaking story, which had been pre-recorded much earlier that same day.

She sat down at the console and flipped on three monitors simultaneously. The Global Access Connection was transmitting, clearly and crisply feeding newslines via satellite around the world. She truly delighted in seeing her own image on the multiple screens. It fed her ego, some would say her ruthless ambition, to be the leading reporter in the country, maybe even the world. If events continued to unfold at the rate that they had been lately, she would be able to write her own ticket. What would that wonder woman, Romie Rogers, think when she, Rionne Sanders, finally had her own network show and pressed that faux Southern belle to the limit? She could go on visualizing her rocket to success for hours, but now she needed to feel the victory of yet another GAC exclusive unfolding.

"A tanker travelling across the Gulf of Mexico suddenly disappeared from radar screens early this morning. Its last location was about midway into the Gulf when all transmissions ceased and it just vanished." Rionne's practiced voice of concern was ingratiating as she continued with her story in studio. Behind her was a file video of the tanker, *Freedom Star*, leaving port earlier in the year.

*Freedom Star* was the newest and considered to be the safest tanker ever built for the transport of oil and any other potentially toxic products. This super tanker was built as a collaborative effort of ship builders and scientists who had been hand picked and assembled by Senator Nash Brookline a few years ago. Since he had a great interest in petroleum production and fuel transport from his early days growing up in the heart of Texas oil country, he was the perfect liaison to make this dream ship come into existence.

Nash had greeted the world press triumphantly when they christened the *Freedom Star* with his dear friend Hy Wells by his side. The ship slid effortlessly into the water, its newly emblazoned blood red, upside down triangle with the initials FS intertwined within its boundaries, shining in the morning sun. Nash had assured Hy that this one ship, and the many more like it that were in the works, would silence the wild-eyed environmentalist groups who had hamstrung their efforts at more petroleum exploration throughout the United States and off its coastlines. At least the issue of oil spills and accidents at sea would finally be squelched, and they could proceed with their extensive drilling anywhere they deemed appropriate.

That was the unspoken back-story that would absolutely not make the news this morning. Rionne knew from years of less than cordial dealings with Nash Brookline that it paid very well to remain on his good side. She had greedily collected the rewards of her allegiance to Nash. Unyielding doors had miraculously opened to her for hardball interviews. Undiscovered juicy photos of politicians or media stars who were falling out of favor would find their way into her private mailbox. She could also count on her email box to be brimming with tantalizing leads almost any day of the week. She knew she must carefully guard this symbiotic relationship. She and Nash knew they both would have much to lose if suspicions ever arose. But enough retrospection, today was her day and she was going to milk these events for all the publicity they could get for her.

Rionne again turned her full attention to admiring herself

on all three monitors before her as she continued her report on the tanker disappearance. "Speculation may prove factual in this mysterious vanishing of the *Freedom Star*. We managed to get exclusive interviews with oceanographic expert Dr. Jale Mindor from Paris. Let's go now to Dr. Mindor." She signaled to start the live feed to Paris and began her interview.

"Dr. Mindor, thank you for agreeing to speak to us at this time. You are aware of the disappearance of the *Freedom Star* just off the coast of Texas early this morning, correct?"

"It's a pleasure to speak with you, Ms. Sanders," Dr. Mindor's accent played over her name. He smiled genially at the camera. He obviously was no stranger to being the center of attention and certainly was quite familiar with Rionne. "Yes, we have been monitoring all reports of this incident. You may not yet be aware that we have placed extremely delicate sensors along the ocean floor in many areas across the world over the last three years. And we have been monitoring them closely, tracking and analyzing every minute movement."

Rionne interrupted, "Forgive me for interrupting, but is that part of the reason that we have been able to so accurately predict the increasing number of tsunamis that have been occurring?"

Dr. Mindor didn't skip a beat nor indicate any possible disturbance at Rionne's interruption. "You are quite observant, Ms. Sanders. It is in great part why your, what do they call themselves, ah yes, The Riders, have been so readily able to crisscross the globe in search of the deadliest challenge to surf. While we are on this topic, may I briefly clarify something about these Dead Man Curls as your young people call them? Technically, they are not really tsunamis but more of a counterfeit tsunami. There is a large wall of water, sometimes over fifteen feet high. And just prior to them forming, there is a sucking noise as the water is quickly withdrawn from the normal shoreline. What makes them different from a normal tsunami is that no sooner do they form and crest, where they provide these dangerous surf riders a thrill, than they diffuse and dissipate to the extent that they do not travel inland as a typical tsunami might. They are certainly dangerous in every way, and since we have no other adequate terminology to better describe them, I suppose the appellation of tsunami will do for now. We are expanding our research to include these recent phenomena as well. But I divert." His confidence again manifested in the tone of his voice.

"Our sensors have provided evidence which I must conclude is the reason for the sudden disappearance of the *Freedom Star* this morning. We noticed some abnormalities in our sensor readings and then cross referenced our satellite imaging." Dr. Mindor's voice became more excited. "What we observed is absolutely astounding."

"Please continue. We are all holding our breath, Doctor." Rionne's comment ignited the Doctor's obvious passion for his research. This was indeed very good viewing and would surely produce amazing ratings for Rionne's show.

"Yes, well, after careful calculations and poring over the satellite images, we have concluded that the *Freedom Star* was overcome by what we can now verify as a rogue wave." He paused dramatically to let the weight of his words take hold.

"Correct me if I'm wrong, Dr. Mindor, but are you saying that there really is such a thing as a rogue wave? I thought that their existence was merely that of inventive fiction writers and folklore?" Rionne was waving a veritable red flag in front of a bull with this line of questioning. And Dr. Mindor took the bait.

"That's what makes this unfortunate event so incredible. Scientists have been studying the existence of these waves for decades and still came to no viable conclusion as to their existence. Since they can be formed from any number of sources, from strong currents, variant coastal shapes, wind travelling over the surface of the ocean, and even the reaction or synergy of waves coming together to form something beyond the singular wave effect, it has made their verification even more difficult." Dr. Mindor realized that in his excitement, his thick albeit delightful French accent was probably interfering with the audience's ability to clearly understand the import of his words.

Slowing a bit, he continued, "Historically, we have come across stories of such rogue waves forming in every kind of oceanic condition, from heavy storms to calm seas, and even forming over large inland lakes. This is part of the history which has allowed these waves to remain cloaked in folklore and fantasy until this moment in time. Now we have irrefutable proof of their existence. However, the *Freedom Star* is not the only casualty today, I am afraid."

Rionne expertly demurred to the Doctor to continue, without even the slightest hint that he had just dropped a sizeable bombshell into the interview. If he had more proof of further disasters, this interview could well go down in history. Rionne Sanders' history, that is.

"I'm afraid that I must be the bearer of unfortunate tidings." Dr. Mindor adopted a serious if not conciliatory tone. "Not moments after we had evidence of this unfortunate disaster with the *Freedom Star*, our instruments indicated another rogue wave on your Lake Superior. A large, privately owned tour boat was destroyed by a rogue wave. And one more incident can now be reported. We have just now confirmed the disappearance of the ocean liner *Precious Star Gazer* in the Mediterranean Sea. We continue to closely monitor all our sensors, but this is all that we are currently able to confirm." Dr. Mindor paused, graciously allowing Rionne to regain the semblance of control over this interview.

"Dr. Mindor, are you and your colleagues absolutely certain of these three incidents? And can you verify that the cause in each case was indeed a rogue wave? Also, please explain to our viewing audience what size wave would be capable of such destruction." Rionne was now in sync with Dr. Mindor and back in control of this masterpiece of dramatic entertainment mixed with news reporting.

"I should have explained earlier. Rogue waves have been known to reach heights of over one hundred feet. In history we had many stories of waves anywhere from twenty to sixty feet in height. Even the smaller ones can wreck havoc. As the wave increases in height, it will often form a deep trough before it. The vessel is then slammed into the bottom of the body of water with such force that there is no possible way that the vessel could recover."

"Could you estimate what size the rogue waves which were responsible for the sinking of these three vessels might be?" Rionne queried.

"At this time, our conservative estimates are from sixty to one hundred fifty feet in height. We will continue to measure and monitor the sensors for further activity. And we will contact you if anything else significant develops, Ms. Sanders." Dr. Mindor had delivered his bombshell and was now ending the interview.

"Leave them wanting more." Rionne said to herself. *"Very well done, Dr. Mindor. I couldn't have scripted this better myself.*

"There you have it. Exclusive coverage of the triple marine disasters that have occurred early this morning with expert insight into their cause. Of course, we are assured by Dr. Mindor and his staff, that there is absolutely nothing to be concerned about for those of you who will be travelling by boat anywhere soon. As the good Doctor implied by the very title, these incidents were probably caused by rogue waves and we are confident that there will be no further reason to fear. This is Rionne Sanders." She signed off. The monitors before her went blank.

*Unbelievable. What a coup!* "I have to get to the gym for an hour or so to work off this adrenaline rush and then plan what my follow up will be. My career has as much momentum as one of those rogue waves the Doctor was droning on about and I'm not about to let anything stop me," she mumbled under her breath. "Maybe I better check my email on the way to the gym and see if anything has materialized while I've been on assignment. This is a very, very good day."

"Let's go, guys," she said aloud to the crew. "We've got fan mail to read." Rionne's attempt at humor hung hauntingly in the air. The van blazed a path back to the studio.

# CHAPTER TWENTY-SIX

THE THEME MUSIC from Romie Rogers' show slithered through the hypnotic stillness of the room. Romie had been seated in a pale green leather lounge chair with her eyes fixed straight ahead of her. The room was dark except for the luminescent glow emanating from the clear glass tank not six feet away from her. She had found herself spending many of her off-screen hours entranced by this miraculous apparition before her. The entire unit in some ways resembled a futuristic version of the antique gasoline pumps that used to stand at attention outside the old full-service gas stations of the fifties.

The semi-conical base gleamed brushed stainless steel in the low light. Proudly perched atop the stand was a four-foot-tall, crystal clear glass cylinder filled with liquid. The liquid would periodically turn milky with swirling undulations that reminded Romie of photos she had seen of the colorful gases that swirl around astral belts out in space. Whatever the chemicals were that fed this tank, they produced clouds that collided with one another forming iridescent greens, ruby reds, royal violets, and every other color of the spectrum. The play of light and color was undergirded with the soft, rhythmic hum of the motor built into the base. The entire unit was cabled to a state of the art computer system with two redundant backup units, side by side. The working parts, the computers, monitors, and motors, were disguised behind an ornate carved ebony cabinet that took up the better part of the adjoining wall. The cabinet had two-way glass doors that allowed for remote visual monitoring of the tank and its contents. Dr. Balfour Divino truly had eyes everywhere. But that was one of the reasons that Romie felt so confident about this arrangement. She was guaranteed that absolutely nothing could go wrong.

As she continued to be transfixed by the light show before her, she noticed a slight movement within the tank. She immediately rose and placed her face very close to the glass. She could see her own breath against the crystalline surface. In the center of this swirling and otherworldly environment, a baby was floating serenely, unaware either of its surroundings or of the tormented eyes observing it through a glass shield. The little creature had everything it needed to survive and become a viable baby girl. It had a constant temperature, a constantly regulated supply of nourishment and even rhythmic acoustical surroundings that mimicked a mother's heartbeat in the womb. It was not cognizant that everything it was experiencing was counterfeit, except, of course the sound of the heartbeat. For that, Dr. Balfour had been very careful to record Romie's own heartbeat. He felt that it was one way to make a potential parent feel more a part of this entire process.

Romie couldn't tear herself away from this aquatic womb and the sight of this baby serenely floating within. This was going to become her baby in a few months. This wasn't going to be just like any other baby with some resemblance to one parent or another. This baby would be absolutely perfect, absolutely resembling Romie in every way. This baby really was Romie in every way imaginable. This was her very own clone child. And she couldn't wait to mold and shape her into an even more powerful and self-assured version of herself. This would be the ultimate challenge and victory. Nothing and no one would stand in her way. After all, what good was all this money, power, and influence she had accumulated if she couldn't buy herself the ultimate extravagance?

Her shrewd business partnerships over the years had provided her the position she needed to make this happen and to maintain the secrecy she treasured in order to bring this baby into being. Between her extraordinarily close relationship with Senator Nash Brookline and her lavish financial and moral support of President Hy Wells, to name but a few, she was virtually assured that this juicy little piece of her very personal life would never make it into the news. No one would dare betray her or cross her in any way. No one dared face the wrath of Romie Rogers. No one.

Her reverie was again shattered by the annoyance of her cell phone ringing. She grasped it and with a perfectly manicured finger flipped open the platinum gold cover inscribed with her black rose without even looking at the caller's identification.

"Hi, y'all. This is Romie. What can I do for you?" she slipped flawlessly into her near perfect Southern drawl.

"Romie, darlin'," purred the very familiar voice of Nash Brookline, mimicking her. "How's my favorite Southern belle enjoyin' her new trophy?" Nash loved to imitate her accent when he spoke privately with her.

"Why, Nash Brookline, you rascal," Romie warmed a bit to the conversation. "I've been meaning to contact you and convey my very personal and deep appreciation for your invaluable assistance in this matter. You truly do have friends in special places, don't you?"

"You know I'd move heaven and earth for you, Romie. It does this old Texas heart good to hear the happiness and satisfaction in your voice. I know that you will enjoy this adventure for the rest of your very blessed life." He paused. "Romie, I'm afraid that I am also the bearer of some disturbing news. It has come to my attention that some extremely sensitive photos are about to be uncovered by a certain female reporter with whom you are very familiar. My people are working on where the traitor may have infiltrated into our midst. But you will have nothing to worry about, my dear. I'm certain that as soon as Ms. Sanders becomes aware of the sensitive nature of these photos, she will be on the phone to me for advice. You know that I have taken that little gal under my wing for some time now, investing in her bright future. She is aware of my substantial influence as well as my substantial wrath."

"Nash," Romie's voice lost every ounce of gentility, while keeping a hint of the drawl. "Nash, my dear friend. You assured me that this very private matter would remain very private. In fact, if I remember correctly, you promised that you would even take this information to the grave. I expect that you will resolve this issue, retain the photos, and any other evidence of this treachery and dispose of it as well as anyone who dared to betray our confidence. I do have your word on that, now don't I, Nash?" Romie knew Nash would understand her comments were more a threat than an idle question. Nash despised being treated like one of Romie's employees. But he knew the scope of her contacts and influence and dared not make an enemy of her. "Romie, I give you my solemn oath that I will get to the bottom of this fiasco and every single, solitary loose end will be tied up or destroyed. You don't worry your beautiful head about any of this. I promise that within forty-eight hours this will dissolve like a mist and life will resume as we envisioned it. Perhaps I won't even wait for Ms. Sanders to contact me. I think I'll be calling her myself as soon as I hang up from you."

Nash's words were meant to be comforting, but Romie wasn't nearly as convinced as she would let on. "Thank you, Nash for your sincere reassurances. I will hold you to every promise. I know that you will be calling me back before the forty-eight hours have passed with some very good news. I am also confident that you will make every effort to heighten your requirements for personal security staff in the future. You realize I have a great investment in your political future, as well as that of our mutual friend President Wells. I desperately want to see you both attain your dreams very shortly, Nash. And please, convey my deepest well wishes to Hy, Marion, and Mercury. Tell them how delighted I am for the miraculous recovery of their precious daughter."

Romie was back in charge of this situation and she knew that Nash knew it. She glowed with her display of power and influence. Her threat was barely veiled and Nash was very much aware of Romie's ability to make good on it. It was a love/hate relationship for certain. There was too much at stake for all the players to allow emotions to influence any of their actions at this juncture.

"Romie, as always, you are every inch the lady," he said with disguised sarcasm. "It will be my pleasure to bring all this to a resolution that will please you. I appreciate your deep concern for the Wells family and I will share your concerns with them this very evening at dinner. I'll be calling you very soon with good news, darlin'." He dragged out the last word.

"I will be breathless with anticipation, Nash." He was dismissed and she was left to her own ruminations.

Perhaps she should take her own advice and tighten security around her residence as well as around the sound stage where she taped her show. Times like these required a deep and prolonged consultation with her long time spiritual guide. She had been meaning to be more disciplined in her conversations with her guide over the years. It had always meant so much to her to know that her mentor Maharishi Mondhi had well prepared her to enter into the eleventh trance where she finally met the Ascended Master who would become her lifetime guide. She hadn't visited Mondhi in several years, but had seen him on the news lines many times as he conducted conferences worldwide, to help other seekers find the hidden truths of the universe. It amazed her as she remembered seeing him so often in the spotlight, that he didn't appear to have aged a day since she first met him those many years ago as a young and impressionable college student fresh off the farm. No matter, she made a mental note to visit him soon. Now, it was more pressing to relieve her spirit of all the stress that she had just dealt with and consult with her Ascended Master for his sage advice. He had never steered her wrong in all this time. She wasted no time and assumed the meditative position she had learned with Mondhi and began breathing rhythmically in and out, emptying her mind and opening her soul to hear from him. The darkness in the room became more intense, as if a black hole had opened around her. The glow from the tank seemed to disappear into this void. A deathly silence sucked all sound from the room. *He was here.* She was entranced and enveloped in his presence. Everything was going to be all right.

# CHAPTER TWENTY-SEVEN

RIONNE VIRTUALLY GLOWED as she strode confidently into the studio and over to her office overlooking the coastline. There were definitely perks associated with notoriety and she meant to collect and thoroughly enjoy every single one while she was on top. But then she was planning on being on top for a very long time. She stood close to the wall of windows that comprised the western side of her office, which was well appointed and reflected her eclectic personality as well as her extensive travels. Many a time she had purposely arranged preliminary interviews here in her office so that she could assert her position and authority on her home turf. She knew every trick of intimidation and was not hesitant in employing them all. As she traced a raindrop scissoring its way down the glass before her, she looked out over the flickering lights of Los Angeles and towards the inky blackness of the vast Pacific Ocean. She could barely make out the lights aboard a few sailboats as they made their way hastily into the harbor.

She had carved out a permanent place in her industry, and she had done it single-handedly, in the most competitive market anywhere in the world. She even had the coveted Golden Pinnacle Award from Micro Global Access Connection. She'd won hands down last year and was secure in making a place on her credenza for this year's trophy. Sometimes it was refreshing to let your mind dream beyond your circumstance. This was certainly the day to indulge. And speaking of indulging, she had a date with a strenuous workout and a soak and massage at her spa. She looked for her travel bag with her workout clothes beside her exquisite mahogany desk with its expansive etched glass top when she spotted an unusual black envelope sitting atop a stack of incoming mail that her efficient assistant had piled neatly in the center.

She pulled out her custom designed leather chair and was about to slit open the envelope when her cell phone began ringing rather loudly in her briefcase. She scooped it out and answered, noting the personal number of Nash Brookline glowing back at her in the low lighting of her office. He was probably calling to congratulate her on her outstanding interview with Dr. Mindor as well as her on-the-spot coverage of the water columns off the Florida coast. She could use a little pick me up and who better to feed her ravenous ego than her covert patron, Nash.

She flipped open the phone and cheerfully greeted him, "Nash, what an unexpected surprise to hear from you this evening. It must be well after midnight in Washington DC."

"Rionne, my little diamond. How are you this evening?" He greeted her with his usual warmth. "I couldn't help but notice your coup in scooping every other news line reporter not just once, but twice in one day. Why that's a new record even for you, isn't it?"

She tried not to gush and kept her voice measured. "Nash, you flatter me. I do feel pretty good about the work today, but I am deeply sorry for your loss of the tanker, *Freedom Star*. There was really nothing anyone could have done to prevent the tragedy. I hope your support of the building of more of these tankers won't be interrupted because of this extraordinary event." The genuine concern showed in her voice.

"Thank you for your kind words. Rest assured that President Wells and I will continue to support extensive new research into improving the design and construction of these monster tankers. No rogue wave is going to stop progress on our watch," he added emphatically. His voice, while still comforting, took on a more ominous tone. "But that's not why I called you this evening, Rionne. I have a matter of utmost importance and security to discuss with you."

"You can trust me implicitly, Nash. Whatever you need just let me know and it will be taken care of." Rionne's curiosity was peaked as her heart rate increased.

"I knew that I could count on you, Rionne. It has come to my attention that you are at this moment in possession of a certain black envelope that was delivered to you today."

"How did you know that, Nash?" Rionne couldn't hide the surprise in her voice now. "I just sat down at my desk and was about to open it when the phone rang and it was you."

"Never mind how I know, Rionne. Just be assured that I do. And now I have an enormous favor to ask of you. I want you to destroy that envelope without opening it. Do you understand? I want you to take that envelope and light a match and watch it burn until it is nothing but an unrecognizable pile of ashes in your trash can. Can you do that for your old friend, Nash?"

Rionne detected a threat and a shudder involuntarily passed through her body.

"Rionne, are you still there, little lady?" Nash tried to regain her confidence and softened slightly. "I know you must think this old cowboy has just slipped off the saddle, but it is for your own protection that I'm asking you to do this favor for me. You can't be harmed as long as you are truly ignorant of the contents of that envelope. There are very powerful forces at play in this situation with far-reaching ramifications that you could not even imagine. Now, I know that every bone in your little reporter's body is probably aching to sink your teeth into this, but trust me, you would regret it the rest of your life. And you have such a bright and meteoric future ahead of you. In fact," he was about to sweeten the pot and dangle something absolutely irresistible in front of her, "I was just at dinner with the President and his family and your name came up in conversation."

Rionne's heart beat now against her chest like a wild jungle drum. She was hooked and she knew it, but dared not breathe until she heard Nash out.

"I know you're curious about our conversation. Well, let me end your suspense. The President has been very impressed with your performance over the years. He feels that as soon as he is elected to the position of Global First Citizen, he will need someone close to him who he could trust implicitly to handle coverage of his new world position. He was inquiring what my opinion of you was for that very position."

"May I inquire as to what you said to the President?" Rionne's voice was just above a whisper.

"Rionne, I assured the President that he couldn't make a better choice. Of course, he wanted some proof of your ability to follow orders and maintain security because of the sensitivity of the information to which you will become privy. I told him that I had just such a request for you and that I was confident that you would prove to be worthy of his trust. Now, Rionne, can I go back to the President tomorrow and relate to him how your loyalty and faithfulness was tested this evening and how you passed with flying colors?"

This was far more a statement than a question, and Rionne knew that every favor had just been called in. There would be great benefit to her, but she wasn't so sure about the cost. Could she risk alienating the two most powerful men on the planet for the possibility of the scoop of a lifetime? Could she possibly even be risking her life for something that was right now a complete mystery? She had to trust her instincts. If this information made its way to her desk once, she could uncover it, whatever it was, again. Only this time she would have all the resources of the office of Global First Citizen at her disposal.

"Nash, you can listen to me light the match as we speak. In fact, I'll flip my phone into video conference so you can watch with your own eyes."

Her voice returned to the confident edgy tone of a seasoned reporter. She took out a lighter from her desk drawer, pulled down on the silver lever and held the flame to the unopened envelope with her free hand. As the flames approached her fingers, she gingerly dropped the remains of the envelope into her empty trash can. Unless she was imagining things, for a brief moment it appeared that she could see the very edge of a photo. But the subject would remain a mystery, at least for now.

"It's done," she said with finality.

"Rionne, you have no idea how grateful we both are. I'm certain that we will find a few tangible means of rewarding your loyalty. And, don't forget, you have a new job waiting for you very soon. I will tell the President in the morning that everything went according to plan. I'll be in touch soon. Good night, Rionne. Pleasant dreams."

Rionne gathered her travel bag and briefcase and set them on her credenza. She turned once again to stare out over the brooding Pacific. The mood of the ocean suddenly matched her own. Mystery begets more mystery, she thought to herself. Well, there was little else she loved more than solving mysteries, and the higher the stakes, the better she liked it. As she stared out over the Pacific, she involuntarily shuddered once again. A random and thoroughly unsettling image invaded her consciousness. She saw herself standing at her office window, much like she was this instant, but beyond her gaze, a monstrous black wall of water was rushing toward the shoreline and then directly at her building. She wrapped her arms around herself and started gently rocking back and forth in a futile attempt to console herself.

What would it feel like to be face to face with a rogue wave? As quickly as this terrifying question eclipsed her thoughts, it was gone. What remained was an icy cold that slashed at her mind and her emotions. She shivered. Closing her eyes, she tried to replace these devastating thoughts by imagining what her life would be like in the next few glorious years. Her mind remained blank.

# CHAPTER TWENTY-EIGHT

BRILLIANT SHARDS OF California sunlight scissored across the floor in Noah's office. All the windows were wide open allowing salty breezes to wash through the entire building. Some of the equipment had already been transferred to the Ark, but only the bare necessities. Many thoughts raced through his mind at once. Would he miss this special place that he and Sara had designed for their lives? Would he ever again experience this glorious peacefulness, especially the ability to absorb the richness of all that nature had to offer? Would he be able to meet and overcome all the challenges that were awaiting him and his family, should they even survive this inevitable and utter destruction looming in the distance?

More and more these random and mind numbing thoughts were invading his consciousness. He was certain that he was not alone in these doubts and fears of inadequacy. He could feel the tension building throughout his little family. The tension had become so tangible that it could easily be measured by the increasing lengths of silence observed when they were together; each lost in his or her own thoughts and imaginings. They didn't dare share these concerns with one another for fear of possibly destroying the delicate seesaw upon which their faith was teetering. Noah had at some time or another come across one of the boys or one of their wives closeted away in a quiet nook, or perched on a solitary outpouring of rocks looking out towards the coastline, lost in thought and prayer. Moments like these caused him to renew his conviction that all this was truly out of their hands and under divine direction. Whatever he perceived his inadequacies to be, he admired his family more each day as he watched them strengthen their resolve and draw even closer together.

He had left the beehive atmosphere, which now permeated the environment between the house and the Ark, to have a moment to mentally review the details for tomorrow. Everyone was engrossed in finishing loading their individual equipment and personal items onto the Ark as well as arranging their quarters for maximum efficiency. Sara was gifted in organization and was assisting each family unit to make the most out of the space they were assigned. She had done an amazing job of overseeing the arrangement of every area in the living quarters as well as the accommodations provided for all the animals they would begin loading early tomorrow morning.

As luck, or divine providence, had arranged, most of the animals, male and female, which had been delivered to Biosphere Five were at about the adolescent stage of development. Thus they would be of smaller stature and require less space and be easier to manage once aboard the Ark. The family was amazed at how many thousands of animal types had been miraculously delivered to Biosphere and were now available for transport aboard their ship. Every aspect of this process had been divinely provided for, even to the almost paved road that had resulted from the "freak" ball lightning the other day. How could he worry in the face of so many small and large miracles taking shape before his eyes on a daily basis? How could he doubt? And yet, those dark moments desperately tried to eclipse the light in his heart. Perhaps this was a foreshadowing of the epic struggle that they were about to witness and participate in? All Noah knew for certain at this moment was that the sun felt comforting and familiar as it cascaded over his weary body. He would close his eyes for just a few moments and soak it all in, then he'd go and help the others finish up.

Every television screen in the house was blaring a different and equally devastating report. And the news lines on each of their computers were trumpeting even more events at greater speed.

News bulletins from Antarctica showed huge fissures cratering through ancient ice flows hundreds of feet thick. As the screaming ice separated, giant eruptions of water geysered into the air. The scene replayed itself in the Mojave Desert as the sand was ripped apart and water began to bubble up from the depths of the earth.

Coastal cities around the globe were reporting the frantic exodus of people trying desperately to move far enough inland to avoid the mammoth tsunamis forming simultaneously. Wherever there was a river, a lake, or even a small landlocked body of water, frightening water columns were forming and now were releasing their own drenching form of destruction as they began to race across the land.

The hapless souls who thought they could find safety rushing farther inland and away from any body of water were greeted by yet another form of watery destruction. The earth had begun convulsing and groaning in preparation for some giant earth-rending eruption. Fissures such as those witnessed in both the Antarctic and the Arctic were occurring also on the plains, through the deepest valleys in the Amazon, across every desert, and throughout every mountain range, wrenching even the majestic Himalayan landscape in order to provide release of this unending flow of water pulsing furiously from the very core of the planet.

As if this were not enough, the heavens began to discharge their stores violently and without discrimination. Thunder rumbled so loudly and constantly that it was as if every jet engine on the planet had roared to life at the same time and in the same confined space. Human ears struggled with the intensity. Lightning strikes played and pulsed and fed off each other without mercy, and human eyes could not withstand the blinding light shows coursing across the skies. The entire planet screamed in unison, retching and grinding against itself as if to shake loose some painful parasite from its flesh. Escape was impossible. No undiscovered patch of dry ground existed that would provide solace and nurture. No man, woman, or child could survive this planetary holocaust. It was a divine symphony, a dirge of sorts. The mourning of the entire earth was about to reach its crescendo. The heavenly baton was raised, the dénouement was now!

"No!" The gut-wrenching scream shook him. *Was it from his mind or his lips?* Noah couldn't be sure and it didn't matter anymore. He had seen what was about to transpire in just a few short hours. The mind numbing devastation was about to start, in all its horror and reality. Thank God, his family would be spared witnessing all the events that were about to unfold. The impending holocaust was too much for any human heart to handle. His was barely beating and sitting suffocatingly high in his throat. The clock was ticking and their jobs were before them.

# Chapter Twenty-nine

THE ARCMANN CLAN awoke early to share what would be their last quiet breakfast together in their family home. Noah sat next to Sara. He found himself memorizing the lines of her beautiful face and lingering in the comfort of her smiling eyes. This wasn't as much a solemn moment as one of steady resolve cloaking the family. The bonds of faith had become steeled over the last months as they toiled together for a common goal; a vision and a future that none of them could begin to imagine. Noah couldn't help but notice that each of his family members had, in their own way, turned their face like flint toward their future and they were never going to look back. *Miracles. My family will become walking miracles.*

"Family, I just want to say that I am very proud of each of you." Noah took Sara's hand, raised it to his lips, and kissed it gently. He looked at each loving face seated around the table. He noted each pair of eyes shone with an inner courage and strength that he had never noticed before this day. He continued, fighting to keep his emotions in check.

"There are no words that could ever express how much I love you and respect each of you." He nodded in respect. "We've worked, we've prayed, we've laughed, and we've cried together in preparation for this time. Our fate is in God's hands. Now, family, let's go and finish what we've been called to do."

They all stood together and reached across the dining table and clasped hands.

"Let's do this!" They all joined together as one voice.

The family piled into the electric vehicles they had been using as transports while working on the Ark and headed over to the Biosphere. The newly paved path created by the ball lightning was going to be a real asset in herding the animals safely and quickly to the ship. Noah didn't expect any resistance from the staff personnel at the Biosphere. In the last few weeks, the chaos that was beginning to rumble across the globe had distracted the powers that be from monitoring and even providing funding for this "albatross" project. And, of course, where there is no funding, there are no employees to worry about. Noah thought to himself that Senator Brookline had dismissed the usefulness of the Biosphere and only gave them carte blanche so that he could get the media satiated while he was maneuvering world focus elsewhere to some new project far more beneficial to himself and to the President.

Even the erratic weather patterns that had surrounded the Arcmann property had played a useful part in keeping the family safe from prying eyes and invasion of privacy.

Noah had noticed that despite periodically experiencing mild versions of the local weather, the space over their property had remained calm. But just beyond their property lines, it was different. The microbursts, rain, and wind made it impossible for helicopters or news vans to make any headway or to set up any gauntlet. The news media became more concerned with their own safety than this crazy story about a scientist and his family building some kind of great sailing vessel on land, many miles from any water. A satellite image would reveal a ten-mile circle of calm around the home and extending over to the Ark, now proudly glowing against the emerald green of the surrounding trees. Yes, everything had been arranged. Miracles dominoed one upon another.

Moving the animals and getting them situated in the Ark had been far more orderly than Noah had imagined possible. When they had first arrived at the Biosphere, every animal had seemed restless and skittish. It took some time for the boys to get the hang of using the electric vehicles to guide and herd the animals along the path to the ship. Soon the entire family was gently guiding this amazing cross section of animals straight from the Biosphere to the ship into their separate pens or quarters.

"I can't get over how calm all the animals are becoming as we deliver them into their holding pens," Shem called out to Ham across the second level of the hold.

"I noticed it too. It's as if they have some internal mechanism signaling them that this is a place of safety." Ham shifted the gate on the pen holding a pair of beautiful colts.

"Animals usually have a well-honed sense of impending disaster and become agitated and immediately seek some kind of shelter." Shem walked past the holding pens on the second level and tested the bolts on each gate. "But that innate behavior seemed to reverse itself once they were inside the Ark. It's really quite amazing, isn't it?"

Shem and Ham proceeded together to the lower level to check on the progress of Jake and Noah. The interior design of the Ark allowed for an open area in the middle, which rose from the lowest level to the ceiling of the upper most level, providing an atrium like viewing opportunity between levels.

Jake was locking the last pen gate as they descended the stairs. Sara was checking the ropes securing some supply boxes in a corner of the third level. Hope, Joy, and Gloria stood arm in arm a few feet out onto the gang plank, looking up at the sky when the rest of the family joined them.

"Mom! Dad! Guys! Come over here, quickly." Joy was pointing

at the sky in the distance. Jake, Ham, and Shem moved further past the doorway onto the gangplank for a better view of the sky beyond the tree line. Noah stopped his inspection on the ground to see what Joy was pointing towards.

The sky, a brilliant azure and cloudless as they had begun moving the animals, was full of rapidly forming clouds churning in their direction. They began as brilliant, dazzling white cotton ball shapes and then continued to morph, building and expanding and crowding one another. The colors became more brilliant but unearthly in their depth and design. Fiery oranges, scarlet reds, and deep ochres fused and stirred and relented into dark, brooding purples and indigo. Each cloud formation was pushing and clawing its way through the proceeding as if in some eerie sprint to an unseen finish line.

The ground began to undulate beneath them, a familiar feeling from years of experiencing the notorious California earthquakes; except this movement wasn't subsiding. Just beneath the cloud cover the distant trees swayed, almost bowing towards the ground and then rebounding to arch to the opposite side. Boulders which had been precariously placed one atop another in millennium past were pushing through the trees as easily as a child's marbles thrown against a wall. They could faintly make out the sound of millions of panes of tempered Biosphere glass shattering and the groaning of steel infrastructure as it separated and crashed to the ground. All sound had synchronized itself into one long frightening moan.

As the family stood entranced, faces turned skyward, a fine drizzle began to cool the ground and fill their nostrils with a familiar ozone-like aroma. Lightening sizzled a path from east to west and back again. The rain began building upon itself, the size of the raindrops and the speed increasing in intensity. Thunder shuddered through the atmosphere and lightning followed suit again.

"Noah, get in here quickly." Sara now stood next to the rest of the family and shouted over the relentless thunder booming overhead. "We need to close the door before the rain gets too strong." Without saying a word, Jake pointed beyond his father running towards the Ark. All eyes looked in the direction Jake indicated. It looked as if two foreboding pillars were forming on either side of the forest where they had carved out space to build the Ark. The shapes seemed so dense that they absorbed any light that might stray into their paths. Before their eyes, solid columns of water formed as a conduit straight from the heavens. There was no swirling like with twisters or water spouts. An invisible pipeline was delivering water at a crushing rate and the diameter of each column was increasing with each passing second. These pillars, which first appeared as sentries to the Ark, were now rapidly descending upon the ship.

The storm was pushing at them, pounding the ground behind the gangplank as Jake, Shem and Ham inched it into the ship. What had once been hard packed earth solid enough to hold the weight of this giant sailing vessel was becoming slippery, oily mud. Small but bottomless cracks were forming beneath Noah's feet as he rushed towards the ship. A part of him flashed through his memory banks in a feeling of déjà vu. His dream: he was running across fields erupting with water and glittering rocks strewn everywhere. Raw diamonds being wrenched from the caverns of the earth by the cataracts of water flowing everywhere. For a moment he was back in his dream, his heart racing, and his legs pounding beneath him as he stretched to make it to his loved ones. This was really happening, just like in his dreams except more real and more final.

The boys had the gangplank partially retracted, with just enough left outside the Ark for Noah to reach with a powerful running leap. The boys and Noah then stored the plank in the pocket specifically designed for it beneath the floor of the ship.

Once the plank was safely stored away, Noah and Jake began closing the great door in the side of the hull.

The ferocity and speed of the monster storm forced Noah's family to strain every muscle. They worked in unison to close the door before it was too late. As the rest of the family struggled to pull the door the last few inches, Noah ran to a viewing portal he had installed beside the door and opened it to see if he could catch a glimpse of what was approaching. What he saw took his breath away. He could now just barely make out the form of the blackest, swirling, writhing cloud just outside the Ark. The sounds of the ground outside as it was ripped apart seemed to crash through the protective hull of the ship. Water from deep beneath the earth's surface was about to meet the vast stores secreted away in the heavens and it was all happening right here, right now!

In unison, they gave one last heave and the door slammed shut. No sooner had this great exit to the world come to a close and the long series of latches been secured, than they heard a gut-wrenching crack. They all jumped simultaneously at the proximity of the sound. This otherworldly explosion of sound was like some unimaginable combination of lightning striking right overhead and the sound of a giant laser beam searing its way into their bones. They could *feel* more than hear what was transpiring outside. The smell of pitch being seared to form a waterproof seal around the door flooded the entire hold of the Ark. Noah looked at each member of his family as they arrived at the same conclusion. The giant exterior door to the Ark was being sealed shut. From the outside.

The adventure had begun. *God help us.*

Whenever I bring clouds over the earth and the rainbow appears in the clouds, I will remember my covenant between me and you and all living creatures of every kind. Never again will the waters become a flood to destroy all life. Whenever the rainbow appears in the clouds, I will see it and remember the everlasting covenant between God and all living creatures of every kind on the earth.

—GENESIS 9:14–16

You did not choose me, but I chose you and appointed you to go and bear fruit – fruit that will last. Then the Father will give you whatever you ask for in my name. This is my command: Love each other.

—JOHN 15:16–17

# To Contact the Author

THEFLOOD09@YAHOO.COM